❧ The Newbery Medal ❧

The Newbery Medal, the first award of its kind, is the official recognition by the American Library Association of the most distinguished children's book published during the previous year. It is the primary and best known award in the field of children's literature.

Frederic G. Melcher first proposed the award, to be named after the eighteenth-century English bookseller John Newbery, to the Children's Librarian Section of the American Library Association meeting on June 21, 1921. His proposal was met with enthusiastic acceptance and was officially adopted by the ALA Executive Board in 1922. The award itself was commissioned by Mr. Melcher to be created by the artist Rene Paul Chambellan.

Mr. Melcher's formal agreement with the ALA Board included the following statement of purpose: "To encourage original creative work in the field of books for children. To emphasize to the public that contributions to the literature for children deserve similar recognition to poetry, plays, or novels. To give those librarians, who make it their life work to serve children's reading interests, an opportunity to encourage good writing in this field."

The medal is awarded by the Association for Library Service to Children, a division of the ALA. Other books on the final ballot for the Newbery are considered Newbery Honor Books.

In evaluating the candidates for exceptional children's literature, the committee members must consider the following criteria:

- The interpretation of the theme or concept
- Presentation of the information, including accuracy, clarity, and organization
- Development of plot
- Delineation of characters
- Delineation of setting
- Appropriateness of style
- Excellence of presentation for a child audience
- The book as a contribution to literature as a whole. The committee is to base its decision primarily on the text of the book, although other aspects of a book, such as illustrations or overall design, may be considered if they are an integral part of the story being conveyed.

Titles in

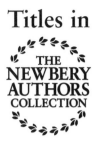

THE
NEWBERY
AUTHORS
COLLECTION

THE
NEWBERY
AUTHORS
COLLECTION

For a Horse

and Other Selections by Newbery Authors

Edited by Martin H. Greenberg
and Charles G. Waugh

Gareth Stevens Publishing
A WORLD ALMANAC EDUCATION GROUP COMPANY

The American Library Association receives a portion of the sale price of each volume in *The Newbery Authors Collection.*

The Newbery Medal was named for eighteenth-century British bookseller John Newbery. It is awarded annually by the Association for Library Service to Children, a division of the American Library Association, to the author of the most distinguished contribution to American literature for children. The American Library Association has granted the use of the Newbery name.

Please visit our web site at: www.garethstevens.com
For a free color catalog describing Gareth Stevens Publishing's list of high-quality books and multimedia programs, call 1-800-542-2595 (USA) or 1-800-461-9120 (Canada). Gareth Stevens Publishing's Fax: (414) 332-3567.

Library of Congress Cataloging-in-Publication Data

For a horse and other selections by Newbery authors / edited by Martin H. Greenberg and Charles G. Waugh.
    p. cm. — (The Newbery authors collection)
    Contents: For a horse/Will James — Touk's house/Robin McKinley — Raising the barn/Walter D. Edmonds — Narrow escape/Will James — El Enano/Charles J. Finger — Deer season/Lois Lenski — Magic ball/Charles J. Finger.
    ISBN 0-8368-2949-2 (lib. bdg.)
    1. Children's stories, American. [1. Short stories.] I. Greenberg, Martin Harry. II. Waugh, Charles. III. Series.
PZ5.F745   2001
[Fic]—dc21   2001031106

First published in 2001 by
Gareth Stevens Publishing
A World Almanac Education Group Company
330 West Olive Street, Suite 100
Milwaukee, WI 53212 USA

"For a Horse" by Will James. Copyright © 1951 by Will James. Reprinted by permission of the Will James Art Company, Billings, Montana.

"Touk's House" by Robin McKinley. Copyright © 1985 by Robin McKinley. First published in *Faery!*, Berkley Publishing Group, 1985. Reprinted by permission of the agent for the author, Merrilee Heifetz, Writer's House, Inc., and HarperCollins Children's Books, a division of HarperCollins Publishers.

"Raising the Barn" by Walter D. Edmonds. Copyright © 1975 by Walter D. Edmonds. First published as chapters 43-52 of *Bert Breen's Barn*. Reprinted by permission of the author's agent, Harold Ober Associates, Inc.

"A Narrow Escape" by Will James. Copyright © 1951 by Will James. Reprinted by permission of the Will James Art Company, Billings, Montana.

"El Enano" by Charles J. Finger. Copyright © 1924 by Doubleday, a division of Bantam, Doubleday, and Dell Publishing Group, Inc. First published in *Tales from Silver Lands*. Reprinted by permission of Doubleday, a division of Random House, Inc.

"Deer Season" by Lois Lenski. Copyright © 1968 by Lois Lenski. First published as chapters 8-10 of *Deer Valley Girl*, Lippincott, 1968. Reprinted by permission of Stephen Covey and the executor for the Lois Lenski Covey Foundation, Moses & Singer, LLP.

"The Magic Ball" by Charles J. Finger. Copyright © 1924 by Doubleday, a division of Bantam, Doubleday, and Dell Publishing Group, Inc. First published in *Tales from Silver Lands*. Reprinted by permission of Doubleday, a division of Random House, Inc.

Cover illustration: Joel Bucaro

Printed in the United States of America

1 2 3 4 5 6 7 8 9 05 04 03 02 01

 Contents

Edited by Martin H. Greenberg and Charles G. Waugh

For a Horse

Will James

Dusty Knight was a bronc peeler (bronco buster), and when that's said about him there's nothing to be took back, for he was at the top at the rough game. Dusty was most always horse-poor, meaning that he always had more horses than he could use; he kept 'em in fine shape, and on one of his horses he could of rode anywhere with the best of 'em and felt proud. If he come across a horse that was an exception and to his taste, he'd dicker for him or work out the money in breaking other horses for him, but some way or another he'd get that horse. It was very seldom that he was left with only two saddle horses, as he was now, but them two was his picked best, and few could touch them for looks, speed, and knowledge with rope and cow work. The other horses he'd let go, as good as they was, wasn't quite perfect to Dusty, and of course whatever little flaws they had wasn't found out till they was worked with a herd, maybe a week after he'd dickered for 'em.

Since his dad had took him on his first ride and before Dusty could walk, he'd rode hundreds of different horses, and always at the back of his head, seems like since he was born, there was the picture of one horse he had there, and with the many horses he rode and the thousands he seen he'd kept alooking and watching for that one perfect horse. He hadn't found him as yet; there'd been a little flaw that went against the mind picture he had in all of the best ones he'd picked on.

He was a couple of days' ride out of town, in the thick of good horse range, where he was always bound to be, and while riding through, going no place in particular, he zig-zagged around quite a bit to always look over this and that bunch of range horses he passed near. Sometime soon he'd strike an out-fit that wanted some horses broke; such a job was never hard to get, not for such a hand as Dusty was. He could prove his hand quick, too, by just watching him handle and ride one green bronc, just one; after that the job was his.

A job was his on his third day out. He'd struck a big horse outfit and where a man who could break horses well could always get a job. That outfit had plenty of horses to break, tough good ones, and it sure took a bronc-riding fool to line 'em out, because they was the kind that was born with a snort and raised with a buck.

Dusty done his usual fine work of lining out the first bunch, and then, when he run a second bunch in to start breaking, there was one horse in that bunch that come near taking his breath away. It was the horse he'd always had the picture of at the back of his head — the perfect one. The color of him was blood bay, black mane and tail, the blackest that Dusty had ever seen, and that horse's hide shined to the sun the same as dark blood that'd been polished on redwood. It was sure a pretty color. But that wasn't the only thing that agreed with Dusty's taste about that horse. There was the perfect build of him, from his little intelligent-looking head to his little hard hoofs. There was plenty of good body in between, about eleven hundred pounds of it, and all a proportion to what Dusty thought a horse should be.

"That's him, sure enough," says Dusty as he watched the horse snort and run around the corral, "and you just wait till I get his round back shaped to my saddle and his neck working to the rein, I'll be mounted like no king ever was."

Dusty was about right. But as perfect as the horse seemed to be, there was something about him that wasn't cleared yet. That was the brand on him; that brand showed that he belonged to another outfit than the one he was working for, to a horseman by the name of Bill Huff, and Dusty figured he might have a little trouble fixing things so he could call that horse his own.

He was more than aching to start breaking him and see how he'd turn out, but breaking him would only raise the value in the horse, and so Dusty just broke him to lead, because now he was going to ride over and see the owner of that horse, Bill Huff.

He found out from the riders at the ranch that the horse had strayed. It was a good two days' ride to Huff's ranch, and Dusty, being wise to men's weaknesses for good horses, didn't take the horse with him as he saddled up one of his own and started over to see Huff.

Bill Huff had many horses; about half of 'em he would recognize by description; but when Dusty gave as poor a description as he could of that blood bay, he of a sudden perked his ears and didn't finish rolling his cigarette before he asked:

"Where did you see him?"

9

"Oh, about a hundred miles east of here. He's running with a bunch of wild horses and I'm thinking he'll be hard to get. I just happened to be riding this way," Dusty went on, "and being I'm circling back now I could maybe catch the horse if you'll sell him cheap enough. I need a pack horse pretty bad."

"Pack horse!" snorted Huff. "Why, man, you'll never find the makings of a better saddle horse in your life. I'll give you fifty dollars to get him and bring him here to me."

That last gave Dusty something to think about. He seen that Bill Huff sure had no intentions of parting with that animal; he also seen how glad he'd been to learn the horse's whereabouts and the relief that he hadn't been stole. It'd been near a year since he'd strayed away.

"Why, I wouldn't take five hundred dollars for that horse," says Huff, "even if he is wild and unbroke."

But Dusty had nowheres near given up the idea of getting that horse. He wasn't built that way. And it was while he was thinking hard and heard Huff say "unbroke" that he thought of a way.

"Have you any horses here you'd want broke?" he asks.

"Yes," says Huff, "quite a few, and the blood bay is one of 'em. Are you out for a job breaking horses?"

"If I can get enough horses to make the job worth while."

"I can rake up about thirty head easy, and if you're a good enough hand I'll pay you extra for breaking the blood bay."

That went well with Dusty. With the scheme he had in mind, even though it would take time to put it through, he seen where sooner or later the bay horse would be his. He loped back to the outfit where he'd been working, drawed what money he had coming, caught his other horse and the blood bay, and in five days' time was back to Bill Huff's outfit.

There he went to work on the first ten head of broncs that was run in, and keeping in mind that he had to prove himself a good hand before he could get the blood bay to break, he brought out all his art at the game. The first few he started got the benefit of that, and in a easy way that made Bill Huff wonder, it seemed to him that them fighting broncs was no more than run in when the rough seemed to be took off of 'em overnight and a little girl could ride 'em. After a few days of watching such goings on, Bill decided that Dusty would sure do in handling his prize blood bay.

And Bill wasn't disappointed. Dusty took that horse, right away gave him the high-sounding name of Capitan before Huff could give him one, and was as careful of his hide as though it was made of diamond-inlaid gold lace. Capitan behaved fine for a green, high-strung bronc and bowed his head to buck only at the first few saddlings. He was quick to learn to turn at the feel of the hackamore rein, and his little chin quivered with nothing, seemed like, only by being anxious to tell ahead of time what was wanted of him and before the mecate knot touched the nerves of his jaws. His little pin ears worked back and forth as alive as his flashing eyes to what all was around him. Dusty still felt him to be the perfect horse, and to Bill Huff he was a dream that'd come to life.

All went fine for a week or so. Dusty rode the other broncs as their turns come, along with Capitan. And then, being Capitan was coming along so good, Dusty told Huff that he was going to turn him loose for a few days, that it would do the horse good and give him time to think things over; besides, he wanted more time to line out the other broncs so he would be done with 'em quicker.

Capitan run loose in a meadow of tall grass for a whole week, and, as Dusty expected and hoped for, that horse had accumulated a lot of kinks in that time. If that pony thought things over, it was towards how to buck good and nothing else.

It seemed that way to Bill, anyway. He was there when Dusty rode him time and again, and there hadn't been a one saddling when the horse didn't buck, and harder every time.

"Take it out of him, Dusty!" Bill Huff would holler, as Capitan would buck and beller around the corral. "Take it out of him, or, by gad, I'll kill him!"

That last would make Dusty grin to himself. He was now getting the horse to act the way he wanted him and so that Bill Huff wouldn't want him. Dusty would let on that he was also disappointed in the horse and act for all the world as though he was trying his best to take the buck out of him. He'd pull on the reins and slap with the quirt, and the pulls was easy and so was the slaps, and, at the side where Bill wouldn't see, Dusty was only encouraging the horse to buck a little harder.

Capitan didn't need much encouraging; it was in his system to buck anyway, and he always felt like he had something off his chest when he done a good job at it. He'd been just as good in other ways and as a cow horse if that bucking instinct had been left to sleep, as it had before he'd been turned loose for a week; but after that week, and with Dusty giving him his head to do as he pleased while Bill Huff wasn't watching, he'd humped up and bucked a little. Dusty could of easy broke him off of that right then, but it was part of his scheme to have him buck, and when Capitan didn't see no objections coming from his rider he fell into bucking in great style. Now it would take a heap of convincing by a mighty good rider to make him quit.

The horse was acting in great shape for Dusty, and Bill Huff had stopped coming to the corral when he was being rode. Bill had wanted that horse for himself, but he was too old to ride such as he'd turned out to be, and he was fast losing hope of his ever being of any use to him.

"He'll always buck," he says to Dusty one day.

Dusty had walked away and grinned. A few more days now and maybe Bill could be talked into selling the horse to him.

All was going fine, and then one day, before Dusty got to dickering for Capitan, a hammer-headed fifteen-dollar bronc bucked too high, and his feet wasn't under him when he hit the ground, but Dusty was. The horse had turned plumb over while in the air and come down on his back.

Dusty didn't come to his senses soon enough to talk to Bill about Capitan. When he come to he was stretched out in the back of an automobile and headed for town and hospital.

He laid in the hospital for a few months, wabbled around town for one or two more, and when he was able to ride again he hit for Bill Huff's.

Capitan wasn't there no more, and Bill Huff went on to tell how it come about. When Dusty was laid up in the hospital he hired another bronc fighter to take his place and finish up on the batch of broncs that he'd started. That new feller was a pretty fair hand and he handled the broncs all right, all but Capitan. That horse had been loose for a couple of weeks and when he caught him he soon found he couldn't ride him. Capitan had kept agetting worse every time he was rode at. Other riders had tried him with no better luck than the first, and when there came rumors of a rodeo being pulled off in town, one of the boys was for taking that horse to it and let him buck there. He was entered as a tryout bucking horse, and he'd bucked so well that before the contest was over that horse had been promoted to a final horse, amongst the hardest of the buckers. Then Bill Huff had sold him as a bucker for two hundred dollars.

Well, it seemed like Dusty had sure done a good job in giving Capitan the free rein. He'd given him so much free rein that it now looked like he'd never catch up with him. But Dusty had nowheres near given up the chase. Capitan was the one horse in a lifetime to him, the one perfect horse, and of the kind he'd sort of lost hope of ever running across.

If he hadn't had the bad luck of a knot-headed bronc falling on him and laying him flat, Capitan would now be his instead of belonging to somebody else and being shipped from one rodeo to another as a bucking horse. It didn't matter to Dusty if Capitan had turned bucker; he was a young horse and he'd get over that. The main thing that worried him was if the new owner would part with him.

It wasn't many days later when he seen that new owner and found out he wouldn't part with Capitan for no love nor money. It was while a rodeo was going on, and when Dusty seen that horse buck he seen plenty of reasons why he couldn't be bought. Capitan had sure turned wicked.

Dusty was in a worse fix than ever towards getting that horse now. But he didn't lose sight of him. He followed him to two more rodeos, and his heart sort of bled every time he seen him buck out into the arena. That horse, he felt, was too much horse to be no more than just a bucker. It had been his intentions to take that out of him soon as he got him away from

Bill Huff and make a top cow horse out of him; he had the brains and Dusty knowed he'd of made a dandy.

Being he hadn't as yet got over his injuries, Dusty didn't compete in the rodeos. He just stuck around. And one day it came to him to ask Tom Griffin, the owner of the bucking stock, for a job helping in the shipping and taking care of the bucking horses. He had to follow along to two more rodeos before he got that job, and by the time he worked at it for a month or so, Griffin was so pleased with Dusty that after the last rodeo of the season was pulled off he gave him the job of taking care of the bucking horses for the whole winter and till the season opened up again next early summer. Dusty was happy and felt he now had a mane holt towards what he was after.

Dusty was alone at a camp that winter. He had charge of sixty head of bucking horses and fifty head of Mexico long-horns that was used for bucking, roping, and bulldogging. The stock run out on good range, and in case of bad weather there was hay by the corrals for him to feed to 'em. He had plenty of grub and smoking and he was all set.

It was during that winter that Dusty went to doing something that made him feel sort of guilty. He was in good shape to ride again by then, and it would of struck anybody queer that knowed the bucking horses, more so Griffin, if they'd seen him pick on the worst one in the string, Capitan, and go to riding that horse.

But Dusty wasn't out for the fun of riding a bucker when he straddled Capitan; he was out to make that horse quit being a bucker and make him worthless as such, and that's what made him feel guilty. He was spoiling his boss' best bucking horse by taking the buck out of him.

The only consolation Dusty had was by repeating to himself that there was lots of good bucking horses and that Capitan was too good to be one, and when the thought came to him that that horse would most likely be his after the first rodeo was pulled off, that sort of washed away all the guilty feelings he might of had.

Dusty about earned that horse before the hard bucking jumps at every saddling dwindled down to crow hops. Spring was breaking and Capitan still had plenty of buck in him, and any rider that could of went so far with such a horse was sure worth a heap of consideration, because few of 'em ever stayed over a few jumps while that horse bucked in the arenas. Of course there the riders had to ride by rules, and it's harder to sit a bucking horse that way than it is when there's no rules and all you have to do is stay on top.

By the time the snow all went away and the grass got tall and green, Dusty was using Capitan for a saddle horse, and what a saddle horse he turned out to be! As good as he'd been a bucking horse, and that's saying something. And now the only thing that worried Dusty was how Griffin was going to take it when he seen that horse come out of the chute and not buck, or would he go to bucking again? If he did there'd be no hope of Dusty ever owning him.

The day came when all the stock was gathered and preparations was made for the first rodeo of the year. Capitan didn't look like he'd ever had a saddle on that winter, and with the care that Dusty gave him — extra feeds of grain and all — he was as round and fat as a seal. Griffin looked at him and smiled.

But that smile faded when that horse came out of the chute on that first rodeo, for Capitan just crow-hopped a couple of jumps and trotted around like the broke saddle horse he was. The cowboy hooked him a couple of times and all he could get out of him was a couple more gentle crow hops. That cowboy had to get a reride on another bucking horse so he could qualify. Dusty was just as happy as Griffin was surprised and disappointed. Griffin couldn't figure out how that horse quit bucking, for he'd expected him to be a top at that for quite a few years. He couldn't suspicion Dusty of having anything to do with it; he'd never seen Dusty ride and it would never come to his mind that any cowboy could take the buck out of such a horse, not when that horse had it in him so natural.

But Griffin wasn't going to lose hope of that horse ever bucking again. He put him in the tryouts twice a day. Capitan didn't at all do at first, but before the last day of the contest came it looked like he was beginning to turn loose and go to bucking again. Griffin begin to smile and Dusty begin to worry.

It was two weeks before time for another rodeo. In that time Dusty took charge of the horses again and held 'em in a pasture not far out of town. It was there that Dusty took the buck out of Capitan once more. It was easier this time because he hadn't accumulated much.

The same thing happened at the second rodeo as with the first. Capitan wouldn't buck, and every cowboy that came out on him wanted a reride, "on a bucking horse," they said, "not a saddle horse."

Capitan began to loosen up some more before the end of that second rodeo; but by the time Dusty got through with him in the three weeks before the next rodeo that horse was scared to buck, and when that third contest did open up and Capitan couldn't be made to buck was when Griffin sort of lost his temper. The cowboys had been digging into him about bringing in gentle horses and trying to make bucking horses out of 'em, remarking that they was tired of asking for rerides and so on, till finally, when Capitan came out of the chute once more and only humped up as a cowboy hooked him, he lost his temper for good and passed the remark that he'd take two bits for that horse.

Dusty was standing close by, expecting him to say such a thing.

"I'll do better than that, Tom," he says. "I've got fifty dollars in wages coming that I'll give you for him."

Tom hardly looked at him. He scribbled out a bill of sale and passed it to Dusty. Dusty folded the bill of sale, stuck it in a good safe pocket of his vest, and started to walk away. Tom sort of star-gazed at him as he did, still dazed by the way Capitan quit bucking after every rodeo. Then, as he watched Dusty walk away so spry, the whole conglomeration came to him as clear as day. He was the one that wanted the horse.

"Hey, Dusty!" he hollered. Dusty stopped and looked back. "You're fired," he says.

"I know it," says Dusty, grinning, and walked on.

Capitan was led out of the bucking string of horses, saddled, and peacefully rode out of town. When the lanes was left behind and open country was all around, Dusty ran his fingers through the silky mane of the bay and says:

"All is fair in love as in war."

Touk's House

Robin McKinley

There was a witch who had a garden. It was a vast garden, and very beautiful; and it was all the more beautiful for being set in the heart of an immense forest, heavy with ancient trees and tangled with vines. Around the witch's garden the forest stretched far in every direction, and the ways through it were few, and no more than narrow footpaths.

In the garden were plants of all varieties; there were herbs at the witch's front door and vegetables at her rear door; a hedge, shoulder-high for a tall man, made of many different shrubs lovingly trained and trimmed together, surrounded her entire plot, and there were bright patches of flowers scattered throughout. The witch, whatever else she might be capable of, had green fingers; in her garden many rare things flourished, nor did the lowliest weed raise its head unless she gave it leave.

There was a woodcutter who came to know the witch's garden well by sight; and indeed, as it pleased his eyes, he found himself going out of his way to pass it in the morning as he began his long day with his axe over his arm, or in the evening as he made his way homeward. He had been making as many of his ways as he could pass near the garden for some months when he realized that he had worn a trail outside the witch's hedge wide enough to swing his arms freely and let his feet find their own way without fear of clutching roots or loose stones. It was the widest trail anywhere in the forest.

The woodcutter had a wife and four daughters. The children were their parents' greatest delight, and their only delight, for they were very poor. But the children were vigorous and healthy, and the elder two already helped their mother in the bread baking, by which she earned a little more money for the family, and in their small forest-shadowed village everyone bought bread from her. That bread was so good that her friends teased her, and said her husband stole herbs from the witch's garden, that she might put it in her baking. But the teasing made her unhappy, for she said such jokes would bring bad luck.

And at last bad luck befell them. The youngest daughter fell sick, and the local leech, who was doctor to so small a village because he was not a good one, could do nothing for her. The fever ate up the little girl till there was no flesh left on her small bones, and when she opened her eyes, she did not recognize the faces of her sisters and mother as they bent over her.

"Is there nothing to do?" begged the woodcutter, and the doctor shook his head. The parents bowed their heads in despair, and the mother wept.

A gleam came into the leech's eyes, and he licked his lips nervously. "There is one thing," he said, and the man and his wife snapped their heads up to stare at him. "The witch's garden . . ."

"The witch's garden," the wife whispered fearfully.

"Yes?" said the woodcutter.

"There is an herb that grows there that will break any fever," said the doctor.

"How will I know it?" said the woodcutter.

The doctor picked up a burning twig from the fireplace, stubbed out the sparks, and drew black lines on the clean-swept hearth. "It looks so —" And he drew small three-lobed leaves. "Its color is pale, like the leaves of a weeping willow, and it is a small bushy plant, rising no higher than a man's knee from the ground."

Hope and fear chased themselves over the wife's face, and she reached out to clasp her husband's hand. "How will you come by the leaves?" she said to him.

"I will steal them," the woodcutter said boldly.

The doctor stood up, and the woodcutter saw that he trembled. "If you . . . bring them home, boil two handsful in water, and give the girl as much of it as she will drink." And he left hastily.

"Husband —"

He put his other hand over hers. "I pass the garden often. It will be an easy thing. Do not be anxious."

On the next evening he waited later than his usual time for returning, that dusk might have overtaken him when he reached the witch's garden. That morning he had passed the garden as well, and dawdled by the hedge, that he might mark where the thing he sought stood; but he dared not try his thievery then, for all that he was desperately worried about his youngest daughter.

He left his axe and his yoke for bearing the cut wood leaning against a tree, and slipped through the hedge. He was surprised that it did not seem to wish to deter his passage, but yielded as any leaves and branches might. He had thought at least a witch's hedge would be full of thorns and brambles, but he was unscathed. The plant he needed was near at hand, and he was grateful that he need not walk far from the sheltering hedge. He fell to his knees to pluck two handsful of the life-giving leaves, and he nearly sobbed with relief.

"Why do you invade thus my garden, thief?" said a voice behind him, and the sob turned in his throat to a cry of terror.

He had never seen the witch. He knew of her existence because all who lived in the village knew that a witch lived in the garden that grew in the forest; and sometimes, when he passed by it, there was smoke drifting up from the chimney of the small house, and thus he knew someone lived there. He looked up, hopelessly, still on his knees, still clutching the precious leaves.

He saw a woman only a little past youth to look at her, for her hair was black and her face smooth but for lines of sorrow and solitude about the mouth. She wore a white apron over a brown skirt; her feet were bare, her sleeves rolled to the elbows, and her hands were muddy.

"I asked you, what do you do in my garden?"

He opened his mouth, but no words came out; and he shuddered till he had to lean his knuckles on the ground so that he would not topple over. She raised her arm, and pushed her damp hair away from her forehead with the back of one hand; but it seemed, as he watched her, that the hand, as it fell through the air again to lie at her side, flickered through some sign that briefly burned in the air; and he found he could talk.

"My daughter," he gasped. "My youngest daughter is ill . . . she will die. I — I stole these" — and he raised his hands pleadingly, still holding the leaves which, crushed between his fingers, gave a sweet minty fragrance to the air between their faces —"that she might live."

The witch stood silent for a moment, while he felt his heart beating in the palms of his hands. "There is a gate in the hedge. Why did you not come through it, and knock on my door, and ask for what you need?"

"Because I was afraid," he murmured, and silence fell again.

"What ails the child?" the witch asked at last.

Hope flooded through him and made him tremble. "It is a wasting fever, and there is almost nothing of her left; often now she does not know us."

The witch turned away from him, and walked several steps; and he staggered to his feet, thinking to flee; but his head swam, and when it was clear, the witch stood again before him. She held a dark green frond out to him; its long, sharp leaves nodded over her hand, and the smell of it made his eyes water.

"Those leaves you wished to steal would avail you and your daughter little. They make a pleasant taste, steeped in hot water, and they give a fresh smell to linens long in a cupboard. Take this as my gift to your poor child; steep this in boiling water, and give it to the child to drink. She will not like it, but it will cure her; and you say she will die else."

The woodcutter looked in amazement at the harsh-smelling bough; and slowly he opened his fists, and the green leaves fell at his feet, and slowly he reached out for what the witch offered him. She was small of stature, he noticed suddenly, and slender, almost frail. She stooped as lithely as a maiden, and picked up the leaves he had dropped, and held them out to him.

"These too you shall keep, and boil as you meant to do, for

23

your child will need a refreshing draught after what you must give her for her life's sake.

"And you should at least have the benefit they can give you, for you shall pay a heavy toll for your thievery this night. Your wife carries your fifth child; in a little time, when your fourth daughter is well again, she shall tell you of it. In seven months she shall be brought to bed, and the baby will be big and strong. That child is mine; that child is the price you shall forfeit for this night's lack of courtesy."

"Ah, God," cried the woodcutter, "do you barter the death of one child against the death of another?"

"No," she said. "I give a life for a life. For your youngest child shall live; and the baby not yet born I shall raise kindly, for I" — she faltered — "I wish to teach someone my herb lore.

"Go now. Your daughter needs what you bring her." And the woodcutter found himself at the threshold of his own front door, his hands full of leaves, and his axe and yoke still deep in the forest; nor did he remember the journey home.

The axe and yoke were in their accustomed place the next morning; the woodcutter seized them up and strode into the forest by a path he knew would not take him near the witch's garden.

All four daughters were well and strong seven months later when their mother was brought to her fifth confinement. The birth was an easy one, and a fifth daughter kicked her way into the world; but the mother turned her face away, and the four sisters wept, especially the youngest. The midwife wrapped the baby up snugly in the birth clothes that had comforted four infants previously. The woodcutter picked up the child and went into the forest in the direction he had avoided for seven months. It had been in his heart since he had found himself on his doorstep with his hands full of leaves and unable to remember how he got there, that this journey was one he would not escape; so he held the child close to him, and went the shortest path he knew to the witch's garden. For all of its seven months' neglect, the way was as clear as when he had trodden it often.

This time he knocked upon the gate, and entered; the witch was standing before her front door. She raised her arms for the child, and the woodcutter laid her in them. The witch did not at first look at the baby, but rather up into the woodcutter's face. "Go home to your wife, and the four daughters who love you, for they know you. And know this too: that in a year's time your wife shall be brought to bed once again, and the child shall be a son."

Then she bowed her head over the baby, and just before her black hair fell forward to hide her face, the woodcutter saw a look of love and gentleness touch the witch's sad eyes and mouth. He remembered that look often, for he never again found the witch's garden, though for many years he searched the woods where he knew it once had been, till he was no longer sure that he had ever seen it, and his family numbered four sons as well as four daughters.

Maugie named her new baby Erana. Erana was a cheerful baby and a merry child; she loved the garden that was her home; she loved Maugie, and she loved Maugie's son, Touk. She called Maugie by her name, Maugie, and not Mother, for Maugie had been careful to tell her that she was not her real mother; and when little Erana had asked, "Then why do I live with you, Maugie?" Maugie had answered: "Because I always wanted a daughter."

Touk and Erana were best friends. Erana's earliest memory was of riding on his shoulders and pulling his long pointed ears, and drumming his furry chest with her small heels. Touk visited his mother's garden every day, bringing her wild roots that would not grow even in her garden, and split wood for her fire. But he lived by the riverbank, or by the pool that an elbow of the river had made. As soon as Erana was old enough to walk more than a few steps by herself, Touk showed her the way to his bit of river, and she often visited him when she could not wait for him to come to the garden. Maugie never went beyond her hedge, and she sighed the first time small Erana went off alone. But Touk was at home in the wild woods, and taught Erana to be at home there too. She lost herself only twice, and both those times when she was very small; and both times Touk found her almost before she had time to realize she was lost. They did not tell Maugie about either of these two incidents, and Erana never lost herself in the forest again.

Touk often took a nap at noontime, stretched out full length in his pool and floating three-quarters submerged; he looked like an old mossy log, or at least he did till he opened his eyes, which were a vivid shade of turquoise, and went very oddly with his green skin. When Erana first visited him, she was light enough to sit on his chest as he floated, and paddle him about like the log he looked, while he crossed his hands on his breast and watched her with a glint of blue between almost-closed green eyelids. But she soon grew too heavy for this amusement, and he taught her instead to swim, and though she had none of his troll blood to help her, still, she was a pupil to make her master proud.

One day as she lay, wet and panting, on the shore, she said to him, "Why do you not have a house? You do not spend all your hours in the water, or with us in the garden."

He grunted. He sat near her, but on a rough rocky patch that she had avoided in favor of a grassy mound. He drew his knees up to his chin and put his arms around them. There were spurs at his wrists and heels, like a fighting cock's, and though he kept them closely trimmed, still he had to sit slightly pigeon-toed to avoid slashing the skin of his upper legs with the heel spurs, and he grasped his arms carefully well up near the elbow. The hair that grew on his head was as pale as young leaves, and inclined to be lank; but the tufts that grew on the tops of his shoulders and thickly across his chest, and the crest that grew down his backbone, were much darker, and curly.

"You think I should have a house, my friend?" he growled, for his voice was always a growl.

Erana thought about it. "I think you should *want* to have a house."

"I'll ponder it," he said, and slid back into the pool and floated out toward the center. A long-necked bird drifted down and landed on his belly, and began plucking at the ragged edge of one short trouser leg.

"You should learn to mend, too," Erana called to him. Erana loathed mending. The bird stopped pulling for a moment and glared at her. Then it reached down and raised a thread in its beak and wrenched it free with one great tug. It looked challengingly at Erana and then slowly flapped away, with the mud-colored thread trailing behind it.

"Then what would the birds build their nests with?" he

27

said, and grinned. There was a gap between his two front teeth, and the eyeteeth curved well down over the lower lip.

Maugie taught her young protégé to cook and clean, and sew — and mend — and weed. But Erana had little gift for herb lore. She learned the names of things, painstakingly, and the by-rote rules of what mixtures did what and when; but her learning never caught fire, and the green things in the garden did not twine lovingly around her when she paused near them as they seemed to do for Maugie. She learned what she could, to please Maugie, for Erana felt sad that neither her true son nor her adopted daughter could understand the things Maugie might teach; and because she liked to know the ingredients of a poultice to apply to an injured wing, and what herbs, mixed in with chopped-up bugs and earthworms, would make orphaned fledglings thrive.

For Erana's fifteenth birthday, Touk presented her with a stick. She looked at it, and then she looked at him. "I thought you might like to lay the first log of my new house," he said, and she laughed.

"You have decided then?" she asked.

"Yes; in fact I began to want a house long since, but I have only lately begun to want to build one," he said. "And then I thought I would put it off till your birthday, that you might make the beginning, as it was your idea first."

She hesitated, turning the little smooth stick in her hand. "It is — is it truly your idea now, Touk? I was a child when I teased you about your house; I would never mean to hold you to a child's nagging."

The blue eyes glinted. "It is my idea now, my dear, and you

can prove that you are my dearest friend by coming at once to place your beam where it belongs, so that I may begin."

Birthdays required much eating, for all three of them liked to cook, and they were always ready for an excuse for a well-fed celebration; so it was late in the day of Erana's fifteenth birthday that she and Touk made their way — slowly, for they were very full of food — to his riverbank. "There," he said, pointing across the pool. Erana looked up at him questioningly, and then made her careful way around the water to the stand of trees he had indicated; he followed on her heels. She stopped, and he said over her shoulder, his breath stirring her hair, "You see nothing? Here —" And he took her hand, and led her up a short steep slope, and there was a little clearing beyond the trees, with a high mossy rock at its back, and the water glinting through the trees before it, and the trees all around, and birds in the trees. There were already one or two bird-houses hanging from suitable branches at the clearing's edge, and bits of twig sticking out the round doorways to indicate tenants in residence.

"My house will lie —" And he dropped her hand to pace off its boundaries; when he halted, he stood before her again, his blue eyes anxious for her approval. She bent down to pick up four pebbles; and she went solemnly to the four corners he had marked, and pushed them into the earth. He stood, watching her, at what would be his front door; and last she laid the stick, her birthday present, just before his feet. "It will be a lovely house," she said.

Touk's house was two years in the building. Daily Erana told Maugie how the work went forward: how there were to be five rooms, two downstairs and three above; how the frame jointed together; how the floor was laid and the roof covered it. How Touk had great care over the smallest detail: how not only every board slotted like silk into its given place, but there were little carven grinning faces peering out from the corners of cupboards, and wooden leaves and vines that at first glance seemed no more than the shining grain of the exposed wood, coiling around the arches of doorways. Touk built two chimneys, but only one fireplace. The other chimney was so a bird might build its nest in it.

"You must come see it," Erana said to her foster mother. "It is the grandest thing you ever imagined!" She could only say such things when Touk was not around, for Erana's praise of his handiwork seemed to make him uncomfortable, and he blushed, which turned him an unbecoming shade of violet.

Maugie laughed. "I will come when it is finished, to sit by the first fire that is laid in the new fireplace."

Touk often asked Erana how a thing should be done: the door here or there in a room, should the little face in this corner perhaps have its tongue sticking out for a change? Erana, early in the house building, began picking up the broken bits of trees that collected around Touk's work, and borrowed a knife, and began to teach herself to whittle. In two years' time she had grown clever enough at it that it was she who decorated the stairway, and made tall thin forest creatures of wood to stand upon each step and hold up the railing, which was itself a scaled snake with a benevolent look in his eye as he viewed the upper hallway, and a bird sitting on a nest in a curl of his tail instead of a newel post at the bottom of the staircase.

When Touk praised her work in turn, Erana flushed too,

although her cheeks went pink instead of lavender; and she shook her head and said, "I admit I am pleased with it, but I could never have built the house. Where did you learn such craft?"

Touk scratched one furry shoulder with his nails, which curled clawlike over the tips of his fingers. "I practiced on my mother's house. My father built it; but I've put so many patches on it, and I've stared at its beams so often, that wood looks and feels to me as familiar as water."

Even mending seemed less horrible than usual, when the tears she stitched together were the honorable tears of house building. Maugie was never a very harsh taskmaster and, as the house fever grew, quietly excused Erana from her lessons on herb lore. Erana felt both relieved and guilty as she noticed, but when she tried halfheartedly to protest, Maugie said, "No, no, don't worry about it. Time enough for such things when the house is finished." Erana was vaguely surprised, for even after her foster mother had realized that her pupil had no gift for it, the lessons had continued, earnestly, patiently, and a trifle sorrowfully. But now Maugie seemed glad, even joyful, to excuse her. Perhaps she's as relieved as I am, Erana thought, and took herself off to the riverbank again. She wished all the more that Maugie would come too, for she spent nearly all her days there, and it seemed unkind to leave her foster mother so much alone; but Maugie only smiled her oddly joyful smile, and hurried her on her way.

The day was chosen when the house was to be called complete; when Maugie would come to see the first fire laid — "And to congratulate the builder," Erana said merrily. "You will drown him in congratulations when you see."

31

"Builders," said Touk. "And I doubt the drowning."

Erana laughed. "Builder. And I don't suppose you *can* be drowned. But I refuse to argue with you; your mother knows us well enough to know which of us to believe."

Maugie smiled at them both.

Erana could barely contain her impatience to be gone as Maugie tucked the last items in the basket. This house feast would outdo all their previous attempts in that line, which was no small feat in itself; but Erana, for once in her life, was not particularly interested in food. Maugie gave them each their bundles to carry, picked up her basket, and looked around yet again for anything she might have forgotten. "We'll close the windows first; it may rain," she said meditatively; Erana made a strangled noise and dashed off to bang sashes shut.

But they were on their way at last. Maugie looked around with mild surprise at the world she had not seen for so long.

"Have you never been beyond your garden?" Erana said curiously. "Were you born in that house?"

"No. I grew up far away from here. My husband brought me to this place, and helped me plant the garden; he built the house." Maugie looked sad, and Erana asked no more, though she had long wondered about Maugie's husband and Touk's father.

They emerged from the trees to the banks of Touk's river pool. He had cut steps up the slope to his house, setting them among the trees that hid his house from the water's edge, making a narrow twisting path of them, lined with flat rocks and edged with moss. Touk led the way.

The roof was steeply pitched, and two sharp gables struck out from it, with windows to light the second storey; the chimneys rose from each end of the house, and their mouths were shaped like wide-jawed dragons, their chins facing each other and their eyes rolling back toward the bird-houses hanging from the trees. And set all around the edges of the roof were narrow poles for more bird-houses, but Touk had not had time for these yet.

Touk smiled shyly at them. "It is magnificent," said his mother, and Touk blushed a deep violet with pleasure.

"Next I will lay a path around the edge of the pool, so that my visitors need not pick their way through brambles and broken rock." They turned back to look at the water, gleaming through the trees. Touk stood one step down, one hand on the young tree beside him, where he had retreated while he awaited his audience's reaction; and Maugie stood near him. As they were, he was only a head taller than she, and Erana noticed for the first time, as the late afternoon sun shone in their faces, that there was a resemblance between them. Nothing in feature perhaps, except that their eyes were set slanting in their faces, but much in expression. The same little half-smiles curled the corners of both their mouths at the moment, though Maugie lacked Touk's splendidly curved fangs.

"But I did not want to put off this day any longer, for today we can celebrate two things together."

"A happy birthday, Erana," said Maugie, and Erana blinked, startled.

"I had forgotten."

"You are seventeen today," Maugie said.

Erana repeated, "I had forgotten." But when she met Touk's turquoise eyes, suddenly the little smile left his face and some other emotion threatened to break through; but he

33

dropped his eyes and turned his face away from her, and his hand trailed slowly down the bole of the tree. Erana was troubled and hurt, for he was her best friend, and she stared at his averted shoulder. Maugie looked from one to the other of them, and began to walk toward the house.

It was not as merry an occasion as it had been planned, for something was bothering Touk, and Erana hugged her hurt to herself and spoke only to Maugie. They had a silent, if vast, supper around the new-laid fire, sitting cross-legged on the floor, for Touk had not yet built any furniture. Maugie interrupted the silence occasionally to praise some detail she noticed, or ask some question about curtains or carpeting, which she had promised to provide. Her first gift to the new house already sat on the oak mantelpiece: a bowl of potpourri, which murmured through the sharper scents of the fire and the richer ones of the food.

Into a longer silence than most, Erana said abruptly, "This is a large house for only one man."

The fire snapped and hissed; the empty room magnified the sound so that they were surrounded by fire. Touk said, "Troll. One troll."

Erana said, "Your mother —"

"I am human, yes, but witch blood is not quite like other human blood," said Maugie.

"And I am my father's son anyway," said Touk. He stretched one hand out to the fire, and spread his fingers; they were webbed. The firelight shone through the delicate mesh of capillaries.

"Your father?"

"My father was a troll of the north, who —"

"Who came south for the love of a human witch-woman," said Maugie gravely.

Erana again did not ask a question, but the silence asked it for her. "He died thirty years ago; Touk was only four. Men found him, and . . . he came home to the garden to die." Maugie paused. "Trolls are not easily caught; but these men were poachers, and trolls are fond of birds. He lost his temper."

Touk shivered, and the curling hair down his spine erected and then lay flat again; Erana thought she would not wish to see him lose his temper. She said slowly, "And yet you stayed here."

"It is my home," Maugie said simply; "it is the place I was happy, and, remembering, I am happy again."

"And I have never longed for the sight of my own kind," said Touk, never raising his eyes from the fire. "I might have gone north, I suppose, when I was grown; but I would miss my river, and the birds of the north are not my friends."

Erana said, "My family?"

"You are a woodcutter's daughter," Maugie said, so quietly that Erana had to lean toward her to hear her over the fire's echoes. "I . . . did him a favor, but he, he had . . . behaved ill; and I demanded a price. My foster daughter, dearer than daughter, it was a trick and I acknowledge it. . . ."

She felt Maugie's head turn toward her, but Touk stared steadfastly at the hearth. "You always wanted a daughter," Erana said, her words as quiet as Maugie's had been, and her own eyes fixed on Maugie's son, who swallowed uncomfortably. "You wish that I should marry your son. This house he has built is for his wife."

35

Maugie put out a hand. "Erana, love, surely you —"

Touk said, "No, Mother, she has not guessed; has never guessed. I have seen that it has never touched her mind, for I would have seen if it had. And I would not be the one who forced her to think of it." Still he looked at the flames, and now, at last, Erana understood why he had not met her eyes that afternoon.

She stood up, looked blindly around her. "I — I must think."

Maugie said miserably, "Your family — they live in the village at the edge of the forest, south and east of here. He is the woodcutter; she bakes bread for the villagers. They have four daughters and four sons. . . ."

Erana found her way to the door, and left them.

Her feet took her back to the witch's garden, the home she had known for her entire life. She had wondered, fleetingly, once she understood that Maugie was not her mother, who her blood kin might be; but the question had never troubled her, for she was happy, loving and loved. It was twilight by the time she reached the garden; numbly she went to the house and fetched a shawl and a kerchief, and into the ker-chief she put food, and then went back into the garden and plucked a variety of useful herbs, ones she understood, and tied the kerchief around them all. She walked out of the garden, and set her feet on a trail that no one had used since a woodcutter had followed it for the last time seventeen years before.

She walked for many days. She did not pause in the small village south and east of the witch's garden; she did not even turn her head when she passed a cottage with loaves of fresh bread on shelves behind the front windows, and the warm smell of the bread assailed her in the street. She passed through many other small villages, but she kept walking. She did not know what she sought, and so she kept walking. When she ran out of food, she did a little simple doctoring to earn more, and then walked on. It was strange to her to see faces that were not Maugie's or Touk's, for these were the only faces she had ever seen, save those of the forest beasts and birds; and she was amazed at how eagerly her simple herbcraft was desired by these strangers. She found some herbs to replace the ones she used in the fields and forests she passed, but the finest of them were in the garden she had left behind.

The villages grew larger, and became towns. Now she heard often of the king, and occasionally she saw a grand coach pass, and was told that only those of noble blood rode in such. Once or twice she saw the faces of those who rode within, but the faces looked no more nor less different from any of the other human faces she saw, although they wore more jewels.

Erana at last made her way to the capital city, but the city gates bore black banners. She wondered at this, and inquired of the gate guard, who told her that it was because the king's only son lay sick. And because the guard was bored, he told the small shabby pedestrian that the king had issued a proclamation that whosoever cured the prince should have the king's daughter in marriage, and half the kingdom.

"What is the prince's illness?" Erana asked, clutching her kerchief.

The guard shrugged. "A fever; a wasting fever. It has run many days now, and they say he cannot last much longer. There is no flesh left on his bones, and often he is delirious."

37

"Thank you," said Erana, and passed through the gates. She chose the widest thoroughfare, and when she had come some distance along it, she asked a passerby where the king's house lay; the woman stared at her, but answered her courteously.

The royal gate too was draped in black. Erana stood before it, hesitating. Her courage nearly failed her, and she turned to go, when a voice asked her business. She might still have not heeded it, but it was a low, growly, kind voice, and it reminded her of another voice dear to her; and so she turned toward it. A guard in a silver uniform and a tall hat smiled gently at her; he had young daughters at home, and he would not wish any of them to look so lost and worn and weary. "Do not be frightened. Have you missed your way?"

"N-no," faltered Erana. "I — I am afraid I meant to come to the king's house, but now I am not so sure."

"What is it the king or his guard may do for you?" rumbled the guard.

Erana blushed. "You will think it very presumptuous, but — but I heard of the prince's illness, and I have some . . . small . . . skill in healing." Her nervous fingers pulled her kerchief open, and she held it out toward the guard. The scent of the herbs from the witch's garden rose into his face and made him feel young and happy and wise.

He shook his head to clear it. "I think perhaps you have more than small skill," he said, "and I have orders to let all healers in. Go." He pointed the way, and Erana bundled her kerchief together again clumsily and followed his gesture.

The king's house was no mere house, but a castle. Erana had never seen anything like it before, taller than trees, wider than rivers; the weight of its stones frightened her, and she did not like walking up the great steps and under the vast stone archway to the door and the liveried man who stood beside it, nor standing in their gloom as she spoke her errand. The liveried man received her with more graciousness and less kindness than the silver guard had done, and he led her without explanation to a grand chamber where many people stood and whispered among themselves like a forest before a storm. Erana felt the stone ceiling hanging over her, and the stone floor jarred her feet. At the far end of the chamber was a dais with a tall chair on it, and in the chair sat a man.

"Your majesty," said Erana's guide, and bowed low; and Erana bowed as he had done, for she understood that one makes obeisance to a king, but did not know that women were expected to curtsey. "This . . . girl . . . claims to know something of leechcraft."

The whispering in the chamber suddenly stilled, and the air quivered with the silence, like the forest just before the first lash of rain. The king bent his heavy gaze upon his visitor, but when Erana looked back at him, his face was expressionless.

"What do you know of fevers?" said the king; his voice was as heavy as his gaze, and as gloomy as the stones of his castle, and Erana's shoulders bowed a little beneath it.

"Only a little, your majesty," she said, "but an herb I carry" — and she raised her kerchief — "does the work for me."

"If the prince dies after he suffers your tending," said the king in a tone as expressionless as his face, "you will die with him."

Erana stood still a moment, thinking, but her thoughts had been stiff and uncertain since the evening she had sat beside a first-laid fire in a new house, and the best they could do for her now was to say to her "So?" Thus she answered: "Very well."

The king raised one hand, and another man in livery stepped forward, his footsteps hollow in the thick silence. "Take her to where the prince lies, and see that she receives what she requires and . . . do not leave her alone with him."

The man bowed, turned, and began to walk away; he had not once glanced at Erana. She hesitated, looking to the king for some sign; but he sat motionless, his gaze lifted from her and his face blank. Perhaps it is despair, she thought, almost hopefully: the despair of a father who sees his son dying. Then she turned to follow her new guide, who had halfway crossed the long hall while she stood wondering, and so she had to hasten after to catch him up. Over her soft footsteps she heard a low rustling laugh as the courtiers watched the country peasant run from their distinguished presence.

The guide never looked back. They came at last to a door at which he paused, and Erana paused panting behind him. He opened the door reluctantly. Still without looking around, he passed through it and stopped. Erana followed him, and went around him, to look into the room.

It was not a large room, but it was very high; and two tall windows let the sunlight in, and Erana blinked, for the corridors she had passed through had been grey, stone-shadowed. Against the wall opposite the windows was a bed, with a canopy, and curtains pulled back and tied to the four pillars at its four corners. A man sat beside the bed, three more sat a little distance from it, and a man lay in the bed. His hands lay over the coverlet, and the fingers twitched restlessly; his lips moved without sound, and his face on the pillow turned back and forth.

Erana's guide said, "This is the latest . . . leech. She has seen the king, and he has given his leave." The tone of his voice left no doubt of his view of this decision.

Erana straightened her spine, and held up her bundle in her two hands. She turned to her supercilious guide and said, "I will need hot water and cold water." She gazed directly into his face as she spoke, while he looked over her head. He turned, nonetheless, and went out.

Erana approached the bed and looked down; the man sitting by it made no move to give her room, but sat stiffly where he was. The prince's face was white to the lips, and there were hollows under his eyes and cheekbones; and then, as she watched, a red flush broke out, and sweat stained his cheeks and he moaned.

The guide returned, bearing two pitchers. He put them on the floor, and turned to go. Erana said, "Wait," and he took two more steps before he halted, but he did halt, with his back to her as she knelt by the pitchers and felt the water within them. One was tepid; the other almost tepid. "This will not do," Erana said angrily, and the man turned around, as if interested against his will that she dared protest. She picked up the pitchers and with one heave threw their contents over the man who had fetched them. He gasped, and his superior look disappeared, and his face grew mottled with rage. "I asked for *hot* water and *cold* water. You will bring it, as your king commanded you to obey me. With it you will bring me two bowls and two cups. Go swiftly and return more swiftly. Go *now.*" She turned away from him, and after a moment she heard him leave. His footsteps squelched.

41

He returned as quickly as she had asked; water still rolled off
him and splashed to the floor as he moved. He carried two more
pitchers; steam rose from the one, and dew beaded the other.
Behind him a woman in a long skirt carried the bowls and cups.

"You will move away from the bed, please," Erana said,
and the man who had not made room for her paused just long
enough to prove that he paused but not so long as to provoke
any reaction, stood up, and walked to the window. She poured
some hot water into one bowl, and added several dark green
leaves that had once been long and spiky but had become bent
and bruised during their journey from the witch's garden; and
she let them steep till the sharp smell of them hung like a green
fog in the high-ceilinged room. She poured some of the infu-
sion into a cup, and raised the prince's head from the pillow,
and held the cup under his nostrils. He breathed the vapor,
coughed, sighed; and his eyes flickered open. "Drink this,"
Erana whispered, and he bowed his head and drank.

She gave him a second cup some time later, and a third as
twilight fell; and then, as night crept over them, she sat at his
bedside and waited, and as she had nothing else to do, she listened to her thoughts; and her thoughts were of Touk and
Maugie, and of the king's sentence hanging over her head like
the stone ceiling, resting on the prince's every shallow breath.

All that night they watched; and candlelight gave the
prince's wan face a spurious look of health. But at dawn,
when Erana stood stiffly and touched his forehead, it was cool.
He turned a little away from her, and tucked one hand under
his cheek, and lay quietly; and his breathing deepened and
steadied into sleep.

Erana remained standing, staring dumbly down at her

triumph. The door of the room opened, and her uncooperative guide of the day before entered, bearing on a tray two fresh pitchers of hot and cold water, and bread and cheese and jam and meat. Erana brewed a fresh minty drink with the cold water, and gave it to the prince with hands that nearly trembled. She said to the man who had been her guide, "The prince will sleep now, and needs only the tending that any patient nurse may give. May I rest?"

The man, whose eyes now dwelt upon her collarbone, bowed, and went out, and she followed him to a chamber not far from the prince's. There was a bed in it, and she fell into it, clutching her herb bundle like a pillow, and fell fast asleep.

She continued to assist in the tending of the prince since it seemed to be expected of her, and since she gathered that she should be honored by the trust in her skill she had so hardly earned. Within a fortnight the prince was walking, slowly but confidently; and Erana began to wonder how long she was expected to wait upon him, and then she wondered what she might do with herself once she was freed of that waiting.

There was no one at the court she might ask her questions. For all that she had been their prince's salvation, they treated her as distantly as they had from the beginning, albeit now with greater respect. She had received formal thanks from the king, whose joy at his son's health regained made no more mark on his expression and the tone of his voice than fear of his son's death had done. The queen had called Erana to her private sitting room to receive her thanks. The princess had been there too; she had curtseyed to Erana, but she had not smiled, any more than her parents had done.

And so Erana continued from day to day, waiting for an unknown summons; or perhaps for the courage to ask if she might take her leave.

A month after the prince arose from his sickbed he called his first Royal Address since his illness had struck him down. The day before the Address the royal heralds had galloped the royal horses through the streets of the king's city, telling everyone who heard them that the prince would speak to his people on the morrow; and when at noon on the next day he stood in the balcony overlooking the courtyard Erana had crossed to enter the palace for the first time, a mob of expec-tant faces tipped up their chins to watch him.

Erana had been asked to attend the royal speech. She stood in the high-vaulted hall where she had first met the king, a lit-tle behind the courtiers who now backed the prince, hold-ing his hands up to his people, on the balcony. The king and queen stood near her; the princess sat gracefully at her ease in a great wooden chair lined with cushions a little distance from the open balcony. It seemed to Erana, she thought with some puz-zlement, that they glanced at her often, although with their usual impassive expressions; and there was tension in the air that reminded her of the first time she had entered this hall, to tell the king that she knew a little of herbs and fevers.

Erana clasped her hands together. She supposed her special presence had been asked that she might accept some sort of royal thanks in sight of the people; she, the forest girl, who was still shy of people in groups. The idea that she might have to expose herself to the collective gaze of an audience of hundreds made her very uncomfortable; her clasped hands felt cold. She thought, It will please these people if I fail to accept their thanks with dignity, and so I shall be dignified. I will look over the heads of the audience, and pretend they are flowers in a field.

She did not listen carefully to what the prince was saying. She noticed that the rank of courtiers surrounding the prince had parted, and the king stepped forward as if to join his son on the balcony. But he paused beside Erana, and seized her hands, and led or dragged her beside him; her hands were pinched inside his fingers, and he pulled at her awk-wardly, so that she stumbled. They stood on the balcony together, and she blinked in the sunlight; she looked at the prince, and then turned her head back to look at the king, still holding her hands prisoned as if she might run away. She did not look down, at the faces beyond the balcony.

"I offered my daughter's hand in marriage and half my kingdom to the leech who cured my son." The king paused, and a murmur, half surprise and half laughter, wrinkled the warm noontide air. He looked down at Erana, and still his face was blank. "I wish now to adjust the prize and payment for the service done me and my people and my kingdom; my son's hand in marriage to the leech who saved him, and beside him, the rule of all my kingdom."

The prince reached across and disentangled one of her hands from his father's grip, so that she stood stretched between them, like game on a pole brought home from the hunt. The people in the courtyard were shouting; the noise hurt her head, and she felt her knees sagging, and the pull on her hands, and then a hard grip on her upper arms to keep her standing; and then all went black.

She came to herself lying on a sofa. She could hear the movements of several people close beside her, but she was too tired and troubled to wish to open her eyes just yet on the world of the prince's betrothed; and so she lay quietly.

"I think they might have given her some warning," said one voice. "She does have thoughts of her own."

A laugh. "Does she? What makes you so sure? A little nobody like this — I'm surprised they went through with it. She's not the type to insist about anything. She creeps around like a mouse, and never speaks unless spoken to. Not always then."

"She spoke up for herself to Roth."

"Roth is a fool. He would not wear the king's livery at all if his mother were not in waiting to the queen. . . . And she's certainly done nothing of the sort since. Give her a few copper coins and a new shawl . . . and a pat on the head . . . and send her on her way."

"She did save the prince's life."

A snort. "I doubt it. Obviously the illness had run its course; she just happened to have poured some ridiculous quack remedy down his throat at the time."

There was a pause, and then the first voice said, "It is a pity she's so plain. One wants a queen to set a certain standard. . . ."

Erana shivered involuntarily, and the voice stopped abruptly. Then she moaned a little, as if only just coming to consciousness, and opened her eyes.

Two of the queen's ladies-in-waiting bent over her. She recognized the owner of the second voice immediately from the sour look on her face. The kindlier face said to her, "Are you feeling a little better now? May we bring you anything?"

Erana sat up slowly. "Thank you. Would you assist me to my room, please?"

She easily persuaded them to leave her alone in her own room. At dinnertime a man came to inquire if she would attend the banquet in honor of the prince's betrothal. She laughed a short laugh and said that she felt still a trifle overcome by the news of the prince's betrothal, and desired to spend her evening resting quietly, and could someone perhaps please bring her a light supper?

Someone did, and she sat by the window watching the twilight fade into darkness, and the sounds of the banquet far away from her small room drifting up to her on the evening breeze. I have never spoken to the prince alone, she thought; I have never addressed him but as a servant who does what she may for his health and comfort; nor has he spoken to me but as a master who recognizes a servant who has her usefulness.

Dawn was not far distant when the betrothal party ended. She heard the last laughter, the final cheers, and silence. She sighed and stood up, and stretched, for she was stiff with sitting. Slowly she opened the chest where she kept her herb kerchief and the shabby clothes she had travelled in. She laid aside the court clothes she had never been comfortable in, for all that they were plain and simple compared with those the others wore, and dressed herself in the skirt and blouse that she and Maugie had made. She ran her fingers over the patches in the skirt that house building had caused. She hesitated, her bundle in hand, and then opened another, smaller chest, and took out a beautiful shawl, black, embroidered in red and gold, and with a long silk fringe. This she folded gently, and wrapped inside her kerchief.

Touk had taught her to walk quietly, that they might watch birds in their nests without disturbing them, and creep close to feeding deer. She slipped into the palace shadows, and then into the shadows of the trees that edged the courtyard; once she looked up, over her shoulder, to the empty balcony that opened off the great hall. The railings of the ornamental fence that towered grandly over the gate and guardhouse were set so far apart that she could squeeze between them, pulling her bundle after her.

She did not think they would be sorry to see her go; she could imagine the king's majestic words: *She has chosen to decline the honor we would do her, feeling herself unworthy; and having accepted our grateful thanks for her leechcraft, she has withdrawn once again to her peaceful country obscurity. Our best wishes go with her. . . .* But still she walked quietly, in the shadows, and when dawn came, she hid under a hedge in a garden, and slept, as she had often done before. She woke up once, hearing the hoofs of the royal heralds rattle past; and she wondered what news they brought. She fell asleep again, and did not waken till twilight; and then she crept out and began walking again.

She knew where she was going this time, and so her journey back took less time than her journey away had done. Still she was many days on the road, and since she found that her last experience of them had made her shy of humankind, she walked after sunset and before dawn, and followed the stars across open fields instead of keeping to the roads, and raided gardens and orchards for her food, and did not offer her skills as a leech for an honest meal or bed.

The last night she walked into the dawn and past it, and the sun rose in the sky, and she was bone-weary and her feet hurt, and her small bundle weighed like rock. But here was her forest again, and she could not stop. She went past Maugie's garden, although she saw the wisp of smoke lifting from the chimney, and followed the well-known track to Touk's pool. She was too tired to be as quiet as she should be, and when she emerged from the trees, there was nothing visible but the water. She looked around and saw that Touk had laid the path around the shore of the pool that he had promised, and now smooth grey stones led the way to the steep steps before Touk's front door.

As she stood at the water's edge, her eyes blurred, and her hands, crossed over the bundle held to her breast, fell to her sides. Then there was a commotion in the pool and Touk stood up, water streaming from him, and a strand of waterweed trailing over one pointed ear. Even the center of the pool for Touk was only thigh-deep, and he stood, riffling the water with his fingers, watching her.

"Will you marry me?" she said.

He smiled, his lovely, gap-toothed smile, and he blinked his turquoise eyes at her, and pulled the waterweed out of his long hair.

"I came back just to ask you that. If you say no, I will go away again."

"No," he said. "Don't go away. My answer is yes."

And he waded over to the edge of the pool and seized her in his wet arms and kissed her; and she threw her arms eagerly around his neck, and dropped her bundle. It opened in the water like a flower, and the herbs floated away across the surface, skittering like water bugs; and the embroidered silk shawl sank to the bottom.

Raising the Barn

Walter D. Edmonds

Tom had supposed building the barn back up would be a long sight slower than tearing it down had been. But it didn't seem to be that way once they had got through laying the stone foundation. The low front part went fast enough, but it took time to build the wall at the rear end, seven feet high, where the barn was dug back into the knoll. Birdy said it would have been a lot more difficult if it had been a free-standing wall, and Tom could see how that was so.

Laying stone didn't come easy to him, but it was something Birdy liked to do more than most, and some days he came and worked on the walls while Tom was still at Ackerman and Hook's. Birdy had a natural eye for stone. He seldom had to turn a stone more than once to have the face come smooth and even with the ones already placed. Every now and then as the wall gained height, he would put a stone off to one side. When the wall was nearly to height, Birdy reached for these stones, one after another, and in a way Tom found it impossible to divine, they fitted in the place Birdy had chosen, maybe with a half turn or a turn, or after a couple of taps with his stone ham-

50

mer to remove a knob or a sharp corner. And as he went along, the top of the wall smoothed out, right on a level with his marking cord. Tom's job was to hand Birdy stones not readily in reach, to lift the heavier ones to the top of the wall, and to mix the mortar as it was needed. Otherwise the wall was Birdy's work and nobody else's. Time came later, when, remembering those afternoons, Tom thought they must have been about the happiest time in Birdy's life.

He kept whistling all the time he was putting up the foundation wall. It really wasn't proper whistling. It came out through his teeth, half a tune, half the kind of hiss a man makes currying a horse whose hide is clogged with mud. But now and then, if he listened close, Tom could make out the underneath side of a tune, like "We're traveling home to Heaven. Will you go? Will you go?" Or something quite different, like "Sparking Sunday Night":

One two three sweet kisses
Four five six you hook
But thinking you have robbed her
Give back those you took.

Birdy's eye would roll around at Tom, looking over his humped shoulder, as if daring anybody to make a remark. Then he would draw a snorty breath, reach his trowel into the mortar bucket, and slap a dose on the top stone, starting his whispered whistle again as he spread it out. Generally by that time he would have got some of the mortar into his mustache, turning the hairs into a gray bristle, so that when he snorted he made Tom think of an old otter telling the young ones to get out of his way.

By the end of August the foundations were done and they started putting down the sills. When they had the bottom sills in, reaching to the rise in the foundation wall, Birdy brought down the two posts of spruce he had cut and shaped on his place. He had decided to make them fourteen by ten, he said, because the logs were plenty big. They would amount to a couple of corner posts halfway down the barn, and he had brought, besides, a heavy girt to tie them crossways. It would make the heaviest cross member in the barn and would help stiffen the whole building.

"Just like a bridge," Tom agreed. Then he grinned. "We'll call it Birdy's Bridge."

Birdy didn't say anything, but he looked pleased, which was well, because getting the timbers into place was heavy work. Tenons had to be made on the butt ends of the posts, and chiseling mortises in the iron-hard old sills was laborious and slow, especially as Birdy would not allow himself to be hurried in any way. Fitting the corner braces took time, too, but in the end it was done, and the posts stood solid.

Then they had the job of raising the girt. Tom couldn't see how two people could possibly get a timber that heavy seven feet up in the air. But it didn't faze Birdy. He managed the job simply, by levering one end up at a time enough to let Tom slide under it ten-inch blocks cut out of timbers from the old Dolan barn. It was slow work, but finally the girt got to its height. The wedged ends fitted into the notches Birdy had sawed in the inner third of the posts and his "bridge" was as solid as any road bridge Tom might ever hope to cross.

After that, putting up the corner posts was simple. Their tenons slipped into mortises originally cut in the sills and they stood there on their own. But Birdy stay-lathed them to make sure they stayed absolutely plumb. Then they put the second sill in place, reaching from the corner posts to the girt and beyond that lying on the new stone wall. The front, back, and side sills were joined by dovetail tenons, needing no joins. As the weight of the upper barn came on them, they just held that much tighter.

They put in the summer beams joining the side sills. These carried the floor joists and were lighter than the great girt. Once they were in, the joists could be placed quickly, thanks to the careful numbers Birdy had insisted on painting on each one. The next evening they began putting down the floor planks, piecing out the broken ones from the Breen barn with planks from the old Dolan barn. In two evenings all were in. The mow floor was complete, and Birdy said it was time to make plans for putting up the frame. By then it was the end of August.

"A barn raising has to be on Sunday," Birdy said. "Or else you can't get enough people to come to it."

Tom said how about the first or second Sunday in September.

"Hell, no," Birdy said. "We got to get the bents put together first. That's why we had to have the mow floor laid. So we could put them together and then we raise them."

"Then how about the third Sunday?" Tom asked. "That would be the sixteenth. We don't want to leave it too late."

"Well," Birdy said, rubbing on his nose. "I guess that would be all right."

"How many men do you think we ought to get here?"

"We could use a couple of dozen," Birdy answered. "But I guess we could make out with maybe eighteen."

"That's a lot of people to get to come all the way here," Tom said.

"Oh, no. Folks always like to come to a barn raising. It's exciting, and if something goes wrong a person might get hurt. And they look to free victuals."

"I'll ask Ox Hubbard," Tom said. "He'd know people. And I guess the Moucheaud brothers would come."

"Bancel and Louis?" Birdy said. "They'd know people in Forestport. Loggers are handy at this kind of thing."

◆　◆　◆

Next day as they were eating lunch Tom asked Ox Hubbard and Moucheaud brothers if they would come and help him raise his barn on the sixteenth.

"It's a Sunday," he pointed out.

"Why, yes," Ox said with his slow smile.

Bancel said, "Sure," and Louis asked excitedly how many other men Tom intended to ask.

"Birdy thinks we ought to have eighteen or twenty," Tom said. "But I don't know that many people. I could maybe get Massey's four hired men to come. That would make nine including you and me and Birdy. We'd need to find maybe a dozen others."

"I get them," Louis said. "Nothing to it. The loggeurs will be coming back into the woods. They stop over Sunday in Forestport."

Tom was puzzled. "Loggeurs?" he asked.

Bancel said with some scorn, "My brother has not learned English too good, even yet. He means the lumberjacks."

Louis nodded, not at all put out.

"The jacks," he agreed. "They will come. They will work at anything. But they are always hongry. You tell your mamma to have plenty of food."

Tom said he would do that. It hadn't occurred to him it would be so simple to find a barn-raising crew. Ox explained that the lumbermen started coming back into the woods in September. By that time they were always out of money. Any that might be hanging around Forestport on that Sunday would be only too glad to come to Dolan's barn raising in exchange for a big feed. They were tough men. They talked rough and sometimes they acted rough. Some people called them timber beasts. But on the whole they were pretty good-natured and they could put their hand to just about any kind of work there was to be done.

News of Tom's barn raising got around. Before closing, Mr. Hook came out of the office to talk to him. He said he would like to help any way he could. Perhaps he could best do it by helping Polly Ann collect food enough. Barn-raising crowds ate more food than it took to stock a grocery store. Once the word spread, people would come from all over to watch. Nobody ever dreamed of bringing food for themselves. They all horned in on the spread laid out for the barn raisers. You had to be prepared to feed a small army.

People came, he explained, because it wasn't often anybody put up a hay barn. It was exciting to see men get the tall bents upright and hold them in place till the plates joined them solid. A sudden windstorm, anything, could happen. It wasn't exactly because they wanted to see anybody hurt — people weren't really that mean. He supposed it was because people were fascinated by seeing something done that might go one way or the other. Like Blondin walking his tightrope across Niagara. He'd done it three different years, but each time it got people just as excited. And it was much the same when it came to a barn raising. People were just as pleased when the timbers were up and solid as they were when Blondin made it to the other end of his tightrope.

Tom figured that the way Mr. Hook described Blondin wasn't exactly true. It seemed to him most people went to the performance expecting, even if they didn't exactly hope, to see Blondin lose his balance somewhere well out on the down curve of the rope. They would see his figure, made small in the distance, fall one way and his great balancing pole the other, and he would go down and down until he hit the raging rapids; and all their lives they would be able to say how awful it had been. He couldn't see how a barn raising would be in the same class, and before he got home he had put it out of his mind. What was important was to get the men to raise the timbers and to feed them and the crowd that Mr. Hook said was bound to turn up.

Birdy Morris had already arrived. He was putting together the bent at the front of the barn. He had the timbers lying on the mow floor and already the shape of the frame showed. At the moment Tom came up on the floor, he was fitting the tenon of the tie beam into the mortise of a side post and finding it a bit balky.

"Must have swelled being out in the weather," he said, as Tom stepped up onto the floor. "Hand me my old commander."

Tom had no idea what a commander might be, but Birdy was pointing at a beetle. It was like a vastly oversized hammer with a wooden head. When Tom picked it up, the weight of it almost dragged him off his feet. Birdy chuckled.

"Kind of heavy, ain't it? Lead-weighted in the head, that beetle is. Forty-fifty pounds. My old pa made it. He used to build barns for folks in his time. Sometimes bridges."

He took it from Tom and swung it sideways, as he might have swung a monstrous croquet mallet. The thump it made on the beam was rock-solid; and the beam's tenon slid home.

"Don't many sticks say no to this old hammer," Birdy remarked. "Reckon that's why it's called a commander."

The work of assembling the four bents went slowly, for Birdy refused to be hurried. Tom's chief contribution was to whittle the pins or trunnels with which the beams and posts were pegged together. Quite a few of the original ones had been damaged when they were driven out or had been mislaid or lost in moving the timbers down from the Breen place. The wood was hard and dry from curing for years in the loft over Birdy's woodshed and each pin had to fit the hole it went into as tight as could be. Once in, Birdy pointed out, it would swell some in the damper air, even inside the barn. It would make an absolute bind. "A durn sight tighter than a marriage vow," Birdy said. A proper wooden pin would never give way. It wouldn't rust out like a spike.

They had the bents assembled more than a week before the barn-raising date. By then Polly Ann and the girls were already planning for the food they would provide. Mr. Hook had driven down from Boonville a couple of times and they had discussed the amounts of one kind of food or another that would be needed. Polly Ann had never been to a barn raising. In the sand-flat country during her lifetime, buildings weren't being built, and she and her family had lived in a house as long as it provided some sort of shelter, then moved on to the next best thing they could find. The idea of maybe a hundred people turning up and all expecting food appalled her.

Besides, as she pointed out to Mr. Hook, she had to keep on with her days of doing housework for her regular employers, as well as the one day doing washing for the men who worked at Massey's. And the girls' school had begun so they wouldn't have as much time to help out. Still, somehow she would have to get enough food together, though she had no idea where she would find the money to buy it all. Her brow puckered with dismay and Mr. Hook, watching her, said he thought the best thing would be for him to consult his housekeeper, Mrs. Conroy.

The next time he came he brought Mrs. Conroy with him. She wasn't at all the way Tom had imagined her from Ox Hubbard's description of an elderly and respectable person. She did have gray hair, but she was a big, raw-boned woman, as tall as Mr. Hook, with a voice you could hear from one end of the yard to the other. It was plain that she liked Polly Ann as soon as she laid eyes on her and right away she took charge of all the planning.

"You've fixed your kitchen real nice," she said. "But you couldn't bake the amount of pies you'll need in a month of Sundays — not in your small stove. No. We'll have to get two or three women in Boonville making pies for you. Not to mention getting meat roasted for your sandwiches. Now I think we'd better allow five sandwiches to a person. Say five hundred of them. That will take a lot of meat, but if you cut the bread pretty thick, sandwiches fill the people faster. Bread. We've got to get enough bread baked. I'll have to go home and figure out the amount of meat and loaves we got to have. Don't you fret, dearie."

"But we can't pay for all that food!" cried Polly Ann. "We are poor."

"Your boy's putting up a barn, isn't he? Then he'll have to do his raising proper. Don't worry, dearie. Mr. Hook will help out." She pressed her lip thoughtfully with her forefinger. "I think I'll go see Mrs. Ackerman. She likes getting into a thing like this. Only she has to be the boss. I'll go ask for her advice, Polly Ann, and in ten minutes she'll figure she's running the whole party. She'll be ready to do anything to make it go. She's that way always with dinners at the Temple."

Polly Ann felt as if she had been swept up by a great wind, and she could only let herself go along with it. She looked up to see George Hook watching them from the door. He looked amused and winked. To her embarrassment she felt herself flushing.

"I'll be thankful for your help, Mrs. Conroy," she said in a muffled voice, and shortly afterwards Mr. Hook drove his housekeeper away. He'd hardly said a thing to her.

"I don't know how we're ever going to pay them back," she said to Tom that evening.

He was troubled too.

"Me neither," he said. "But I don't know no other way we'll get the barn raised."

Then, seeing she wasn't reassured at all, he added, "We'll pay them some way."

But he could hardly believe it himself.

◆ ◆ ◆

That last week before the raising was so full of women coming and going that Tom always spoke of it, even long afterwards, as the most mixed-up time in his life. He didn't see how anything would come out of so much commotion. Polly Ann got only the most skimpy kind of scratch suppers, after which she would whirl into making bread or baking pies. By Saturday she had what seemed to Tom a pretty good stock of loaves and pies laid up in the cold pantry off the kitchen; but when he remarked so, she said, "Goodness, those aren't only a drop in the bucket."

She had him put a hook on the door so the cats couldn't get in and make trouble. That last Saturday she cooked the biggest jar of doughnuts Tom or his sisters ever saw. It was hard to believe.

Late in the afternoon, after the mill closed down, Mr. Hook drove Mrs. Conroy down from town in a buckboard he had rented from Joe Hemphill's livery because she had more food to bring than his buggy could accommodate. There were three roasts of beef and the biggest turkey bird Tom had ever seen, and two large fresh hams, racks of pies, and loaves of bread as well. When it was all stacked up in the pantry it looked big enough, with what Polly Ann had already cooked, to feed an army. Mrs. Conroy shook her head, but she said Mrs. Ackerman was coming in the morning with additional supplies, and with those she thought they might get by.

She then wanted to see what Polly Ann had done about providing serving tables. Birdy had brought four sawhorses from his own place. With the two Tom had and planks from the old barn there would be three tables which they had supposed would be enough, but Mrs. Conroy wanted a fourth. So Tom said he would see if he could borrow two more saw-horses from Massey, down the road. He walked down after supper and Massey was agreeable. He led Tom into the barn to get them, and Tom looked enviously at the two lines of big Holstein cows in their iron stanchions, standing on the concrete floor. He wouldn't be able to afford anything like that for a long time. But when Massey said, "I hear you've got a real good barn," he agreed.

"Just the timbers, really, though," he told Massey.

He picked up the horses, one to each shoulder and Massey said, "See you tomorrow, Tom. I'm coming up with the boys. There's nothing makes a man feel better than seeing a barn raised."

It made Tom feel better. It was a nice thing for Mr. Massey to say, considering what a great lot larger his own barn was than Tom's. And Mr. Massey added, "We'll bring up the pike poles we used raising this barn, Tom. You can't ever have too many if you've got the men on hand to use them."

Tom said his thanks. And walking home he thought how he had first seen the barn at Widow Breen's and remembered the old lady standing on her porch, pointing her shotgun at him. That was when he had got the notion of moving the barn, but it didn't seem likely then that it would ever get as far along as this.

Birdy had stayed for supper, but he had gone by the time Tom got home, leaving word with Polly Ann that he would be down early next morning, to make sure that everything was how it should be, and for Tom not to worry.

But, of course, Tom did. He and Polly Ann sat in the kitchen to have a cup of tea together and he could see she was as worried as he was. It was the money they were going to owe that bothered both of them. Birdy wasn't worried that way. It wasn't him getting into debt, naturally; but then he never worried about money anyway.

Cissie-Mae and Ellie came into the kitchen, but seeing their Ma and Tom so silent took themselves off to bed after a minute or two. After that there wasn't anything to hear but the late crickets fiddling in the meadow beyond the barnyard. So pretty soon they, too, went up to bed.

For a long time, however, bed wasn't a place for going to sleep. Tom got too hot and threw the covers off, and then after a while he got too cold. No matter what he kept on top of him, he couldn't get things right. When he dozed off, at last, a mouse gnawing inside the wall woke him, and then that changed into a dream of a great mouse chewing off the bottoms of the bents as fast as they could get them upright, so they never had two of them raised at one time long enough to join. That woke him right up and he was sweating again, but this time he felt cold. He pulled the quilt up and curled up under it, and suddenly he felt himself sliding off to sleep, but at the last instant it came into his mind how awful it would be should it come on to rain next day.

◆ ◆ ◆

When he woke, he kept his eyes closed for a minute; but there was no sound of rain. So he opened them to a brilliant sunrise and at once got up. He had barely finished washing on the kitchen stoop when he heard the sound of a wagon coming along their road, and a minute later Birdy Morris drove into the yard. Birdy waved as he drove by to a place behind the milking shed. At the same time Polly Ann rattled wood into the kitchen stove and upstairs he heard Ellie's voice complaining querulously that it was too early. Over at the edge of the yard one of the hens announced the arrival of an egg as if it were a wonder of the world. The brightening sunlight touched the mow floor where the assembled bents lay flat and Tom tried to remember just how they had looked, standing bare as bones up at the Widow Breen's place, before he and Birdy took them down.

After unhitching his horses, Birdy came back to the house and admitted he could drink a cup of coffee, and then he confessed that he had left home without eating anything. He had been troubled that they might not have enough pike poles, so Tom was able to ease his mind by saying that Massey had said he would bring the ones he had used raising his own barn.

It was warm enough for them to eat breakfast with the kitchen door open. Birdy even unbuttoned the collar of his shirt and Tom noticed for the first time that it was brand-new gray flannel with a thin green stripe. He wondered if Birdy had bought it just for the barn raising. Cissie-Mae and Ellie clattered down the stairs and came sleepily into the kitchen. Polly Ann told them to be quick: there was more than plenty of things for them to do. As they went over to the stove, drumming hoofs sounded down the road with a whir of wheels, and Mr. Hook swung the big gray into the yard, stopping his buggy by the kitchen steps. Mrs. Conroy got down lugging a monumental coffee kettle; and Tom realized that his barn-raising day was really under way.

Afterwards it seemed to him that he hadn't had much of anything to do with the program. For a time Mrs. Conroy monopolized almost everybody — getting the tables set up on the sawhorses; showing just where she wanted them placed, as much in the shade as possible, since the sun promised to be hot and the sandwiches might dry out. Then she had Polly Ann and the girls go to work slicing bread in the kitchen for the sandwiches. They worked in a fine smell of coffee, which drifted out across the yard all the way to the barn. About nine-thirty they began coming out with platters stacked with the sandwiches and six huge pans of cold baked white beans, each with its own cruet of vinegar and an arrangement of separate plates and forks. When these were all positioned, they placed pies at intervals, each with a pie knife beside it.

By then the men were starting to show up. Massey came with his four hired hands, carrying pike poles on their shoulders as they walked up the road.

"Thought there'd be rigs enough around the place without ours," Massey said.

All the others arrived in wagons. First came the Moucheauds, riding together with Louis's wife and children, not to mention some relations. There were fourteen of them, and the moment the children got their feet on the ground they took off on the run, going all over the place, this way and that, like small chickens. It was impossible to keep track of them. Tom figured they would have had half the sandwiches eaten in no time if Mrs. Conroy hadn't taken up a guard post with a buggy whip which she wasn't at all afraid to use.

All of a sudden the Moucheaud children were distracted by a clamor on the road. Not exactly a hullabaloo, not exactly yelling, just a good-humored uproar; it prompted Louis to declare they must be the loggeurs from Forestport.

"He means the lumberjacks," Bancel said scornfully, as he had before.

They wheeled into the yard in two buckboards, one a three-seater, the other a four-seater. There were thirteen men dressed in heavy shirts like coats with cotton shirts underneath and wearing every kind of hat you could imagine. They shouted greetings at the Moucheauds, who brought them over to Tom to be introduced, and they expressed astonishment that a boy like him should be putting up a barn for himself.

"Don't worry," they said. "We'll put them bents up. Even if we have to toss them up with our hands."

"How about tapping one of those barr'ls?" another suggested, and Tom saw that each buckboard had a keg lashed on the tailboard. But the one who had first talked to Tom said, "Not until we have these timbers up." He turned to Tom. "The boys brought along the drink because it was Sunday. No offense intended to you or your mamma."

Tom said all he wanted was to get the frame raised. He hoped they would like the lunch that had been laid out.

Mr. Hook came off the kitchen porch just then with a couple of pails of switchel, which he put down near the barn.

"Mrs. Dolan thought this would help keep your thirst down, for now," he said. Each bucket had a dipper floating in it, and the lumberjacks took turns drinking from them with the hired men from Massey's. There was considerable talk about how hot the day was likely to be, mostly to justify this early assault on the switchel. By the time Birdy and Mr. Massey came over to join them, everybody was feeling amiable.

Mr. Massey introduced Birdy to them.

"Birdy Morris is the man who built this barn in the first place. For Bert Breen, up on the sand flats by the Forestport line. He's helped Tom Dolan take it down and bring it here. I'd say he was the man to be caller for us."

Lumberjacks didn't step to one side for anybody, but they recognized boss material when they met it, and though Birdy didn't look like much, with his humped shoulder and all, they agreed he ought to be their man.

Birdy nodded soberly.

"Well," he said, "I guess we might as well commence."

As they moved towards the barn, three more wagons drove in. Two were from Port Leyden, with three men, three wives, and seven children between them. The other was from Potato Hill and brought three single men. All six men had brought pike poles with them, so Birdy's anxieties on this matter were quieted for good. They all introduced themselves and joined the men moving towards the barn. The whole group filed up the stairs to the mow floor or climbed the ladders leaning against. it.

Birdy's first move was to have the pike poles laid out in some sort of order, the short ones in one rank and the twelve-footers in another. He suggested that Ox Hubbard and one of the men from Port Leyden take charge of the planting of each post of the first bent. There were heavy blocks to keep it from slipping off as it went up. Ox and the Port Leyden man, whose name was Hennessy, had stay laths ready to fix the bent as soon as it stood plumb and each had a couple of helpers with hammers and spikes. After it was in position, the braces would be put in and pinned.

The first step of the raising was done with the men's hands. They had to get the bent head high before the short pikes could be used. Those first feet upwards were the hardest part of the whole job. Half the men hooked their hands under the tie beam and braced their feet, their eyes on Birdy Morris, who stood at the center of the mow floor underneath where the tie beam would be once it was full up. He gave his mustache a wipe with his forefinger. Then his voice sounded, much bigger than you would expect.

"Hee-yo — HEAVE!"

At the word, the men lifted all together and the bent rose slowly with the butts of its posts against the end blocks. The men held it just over their heads and Tom, at his place in the line, felt a tremor in the bent. It didn't surprise him. His own arms were trembling with the strain. But then the men with the short poles sank their pike picks in the tie beam, taking up the weight, while Tom and his team stepped back. Already a lot of them were showing sweat marks on their shirts.

Birdy's voice came again.

"Hee-yo — HEAVE!"

The bent rose higher. The first group grabbed up the twelve-foot poles and sank their pike picks into the beam between those of the short-pole crew.

At Birdy's call, they heaved again. Ox's voice sounded calmly over their labored breathing. "She's up."

Hennessy from Port Leyden echoed him. Seven men on the ground outside the barn, waiting with still longer poles, sank the picks into the beam and held it steady against those of the men on the mow floor. Ox and Hennessy raised the end of the stay laths which had already been single-spiked on the outside of the second sill with enough overlap to give a bite head-high on the post. They put their levels against the post and called for a little more pressure from the outside pike poles, and suddenly their hammers sounded together. They drove two more spikes into the post, and then, at the other end of the laths, into the second sills.

The first bent stood properly erect.

◆ ◆ ◆

The beams to connect the bents were next to put in place. Men raised them until their tenons entered the mortises in the posts. A rope from the end of each was passed over the tie beam and two men on the ground took hold of the end, keeping the beam horizontal to meet the next bent when it was raised. The pike-pole crews were still around the switchel pails. Birdy shouted for them to come back to the job. It was time to raise the second bent. At that moment the fringed surrey from Hemphill's livery wheeled into the yard. Joe Hemphill himself was driving; it was less than a year old and he was choosy about renting it out for anyone else to drive. He was wearing his derby hat, which he only did on occasions of importance and Tom at once saw why. On the back seat were Erlo and Mrs. Ackerman.

Mrs. Ackerman was built as solid as Erlo and looked more so on account of the hat she was wearing — stiff with a multitude of ribbons. As they got out, first one and then the other, the surrey rocked from side to side like a boat in the trough of a wave. Erlo made for the kitchen porch and settled himself in a rocker right at the top of the steps, where he would have an uninterrupted view. Polly Ann brought him a glass of switchel but he asked for coffee so she brought him a cup and small side table from the parlor to put it on. Mrs. Ackerman meanwhile was going down the tables checking on everything there was under the cheesecloth with Mrs. Conroy accompanying her. The Moucheaud children, now joined by a dozen others, considered this a good time to stage a raid at the far end of the farthest table; but they hadn't counted on Mrs. Conroy's agility. She caught them with their hands under the cloth and got in a couple of licks with the buggy whip that sent them off yelping like puppies.

The commotion temporarily put a stop to the raising. Nobody seemed to mind, except the men on the ropes holding up the connecting beams, who made jokes about staying as they were till the barn got shingled or what would they do if a couple of them died of old age. Tom came down to make his manners to Mrs. Ackerman, who took no notice of him, and then he said hello to Erlo.

"You got things going good," Erlo told him. "I'm sorry we're late, but don't pay attention to us. The barn's what's important, Tom."

Things got going quickly then. The second bent went up as smoothly as the first. The tenons of the connecting beams found their mortises with very little difficulty. It was plain that Ox and the men working with him knew what they were about. The work went on well. They had the third bent up and locked in place a little after noon and decided to knock off and eat.

This was not only the moment Polly Ann, Mrs. Conroy, and the other women had been preparing for, it was the one the children had been waiting for almost to the point of desperation. All in an instant twenty or thirty small hands were grabbing and the sandwiches melted away like feasts in dreams. As soon as they had snatched their food the children would rush off somewhere out of sight, but in a few minutes they came tearing back, all in a bunch, like swarming bees.

The men helped themselves to stacks of the sandwiches, to hunks of cheese, to cherry or blueberry or apple pie, and drank quantities of coffee and switchel. They ignored the gyrations of the mob of children or tolerated them good-humoredly, perhaps remembering other barn raisings when they themselves had been small. They kept in separate groups, the lumberjacks sitting by themselves in the shade of the house, the farmers under the mow floor. The Moucheaud brothers circulated from one group to the other. Working at the feed mill and living in Forestport made them parties of both worlds. Tom, feeling himself the host, tried to do the same, but he felt shy among the lumberjacks and found little to say to them.

Mr. Massey came up to him and said that the raising seemed to have gone well. "Looks like you have a good sound barn, there," he said. "We'll be glad to come another Sunday and help put the roof on."

Tom said he would appreciate the help and led Mr. Massey up on the porch to where Erlo Ackerman was sitting. Massey was, naturally, one of Erlo's biggest customers and was welcomed accordingly. Suddenly, in the windless, warm noon, the party seemed as peaceful as a church sociable. Tom took some sandwiches from Cissie-Mae and sat down on the steps near Mr. Hook.

"It looks as if everything's going well, Tom," Mr. Hook said.

"Yes," Tom said. "But there's going to be an awful lot to do after we get the frame up."

"Erlo and I were talking about that. We thought maybe you would like to take a week off from the mill. Maybe two. Of course," Mr. Hook added, "that would be without pay. Erlo wanted to make that plain."

"It might be a good idea," Tom said. "Only I've got to make money anyways I can. I've got to find money for the shingles and the siding somehow."

"I'd be glad to make you a loan, Tom. If you want one."

Tom thought about it. He had an uneasy feeling that Polly Ann wouldn't like him to take money from Mr. Hook. Even loan money. He said, "Thanks," because he had to. But he didn't know what was right. He said, "I'll let you know, Mr. Hook, if I have to have it."

"Think about it, anyway, Tom."

They sat silent, watching the people moving around the yard. The children suddenly appeared from the far side of the house, still running bunched up. They were after pie or cake and it took some active work on the part of Mrs. Conroy, Polly Ann, and Cissie-Mae to cut them all pieces before they made grabs for an entire pie. Mrs. Ackerman didn't approve of giving them any. She said the manners of children had got worse ever since she was a girl.

Mr. Hook smiled lazily, and then he said, "Who's that man under the barn floor with Ox, Tom? I saw him a couple of minutes ago talking to Massey. But I didn't see him here at all before then."

There wasn't any mistaking who it was.

"That's Yantis Flancher," Tom told him. "He's got two brothers. They generally always go together."

"He looks like a rough character."

"I guess he is. Him and his brothers have been up at Breen's most of the time this summer. Looking for Mr. Breen's money."

"Did they make any trouble for you?" Mr. Hook asked.

Tom shook his head. "Just told me not to go hunting for the money myself."

Tom told him how Yantis and his brothers, Newman and Enders, had ripped the walls of the house apart and dug trenches all over the place.

"I don't see what he wants to come here for," Mr. Hook said.

Tom grinned thinly. "Checking up on me, I guess. Wondering if maybe I have found that money."

"You'd think," Mr. Hook said, "somebody'd have found the money by now, if it was there."

"Yes, you would," Tom said.

He got up. Birdy Morris was climbing up on the mow floor and Tom wanted to talk to Ox before they started work again.

Ox said, "Yantis was asking me why you and Birdy hadn't put the cattle floor down yet. I told him I didn't know. You was doing the job your own way."

Mr. Massey came up to them. "He asked me the same thing. Did I know why? Said it seemed a queer way to put up a barn. I told him maybe you were figuring to lay a cement floor, like my barn."

"What did he say?"

"He wanted to know where you were going to find the money to pay for a cement floor. I didn't know. I said that was your business." Massey smiled. "He didn't like me saying that. I could see he didn't like me. But then I didn't like him, either."

Birdy called them then. The men trooped back. Tom looked past the house to the road. He saw the Flanchers' wagon driving off, heading downriver towards Port Leyden.

Yantis's brothers, Newman and Enders, were with him. He figured they must be going back home to Highmarket.

◆ ◆ ◆

The last bent went up quickly, without a hitch. The job was made simpler by the knoll into which the barn had been dug. The men raising the bent were standing on ground level with the mow floor.

After it was standing, the farmers started leaving. They had their own evening chores coming up. But the Moucheauds and the lumberjacks stayed on, helping to put up the plates, the beams joining the top corners of the bents, on which the rafters would rest. The lumbermen were like cats running back and forth along the beams and with Ox Hubbard and Birdy supervising, the plates were fixed in short order. The frame was raised and the shape of the barn stood there for anyone to see. It looked bigger to Tom than it had up on the Breen place.

Louis Moucheaud put the longest ladder up to one of the top posts of the bent facing the house and climbed it, carrying a small balsam tree. He fastened it there with a length of twine, the "brush" to bring luck to the barn. The men raised a cheer and came tumbling down off the frame. They got their kegs off the buckboards, drove the bungs, and in no time every man had a dipper, glass, or mug of frothing beer. Erlo Ackerman came down the steps of the kitchen porch and joined them.

They drank to the barn's future and to Tom, who was tasting beer for the first time in his life and not liking it at all. After the second or third round, one of them began to sing, a sad haunting kind of tune in which the Moucheauds joined. It was a song from Canada, somebody said, and the reason Tom and most of the others couldn't make out the words was because they were French. It was another half hour before they were ready to leave, and even then it took a while to round up the Moucheaud children. But at last they were gone.

Mrs. Conroy helped Polly Ann and the girls to clear up while Mrs. Ackerman offered advice. But then she came over to Erlo and said it was time for them to leave, too. They had to hunt up Joe Hemphill, who had gone to sleep on the old settee at the end of the front porch. Tom had some difficulty rousing him. His breath was strong, but not with beer, so Tom guessed that he must have brought something stronger with him as a precaution. Livery men were known to have precautious instincts. He got Joe up on his feet, which showed a reluctance to move in the same direction, but by the time they had reached the fringed surrey he was navigating to some purpose, and when the Ackermans climbed on board, Tom felt no anxiety about their getting back to Boonville. Joe Hemphill's horses knew the way home better than he did.

He returned to the back of the house to find that the tables had been stripped. Mr. Hook was carrying the planks back to the pile they had come from. Tom put his own sawhorses away and took the four Birdy had brought to Birdy's wagon. The old man had gone back to the mow floor. He stood in the middle of it looking up at the timbers, back together in their proper shape, the way he had helped fix them in the first place. A long time, that was. He wondered what Bert Breen would think to see them down here. Or Amelie, either.

Then he saw Tom and Mr. Hook approaching him, and he came down the ladder.

"I got to get back home, Tom," he said. "But the raising went good, didn't it?"

"It did," Tom said. "Thanks mostly to you, Birdy."

Birdy looked embarrassed, especially when George Hook put in his word of agreement.

"Pshaw," he said. "Raising a barn ought to go good, when it's the second time around."

He got into his wagon and drove the team slowly through the yard. He took his hat off when he passed Mrs. Conroy and Polly Ann.

"Been a good day," he told them.

"Yes," Polly Ann said. "Thank you, Birdy, for all the things you've done for Tom. For us all."

"Pshaw," he said again. "We've got to roof it yet, and put the siding on."

He drove out on to the road. One of his wheels started to squeak. Tom said to Mr. Hook that he had never known Birdy to let an axle go dry. Then he realized that he hadn't looked at his own wagon either for too long. That was something he couldn't leave a minute longer. But he had to wait till Mrs. Conroy was ready to go and Mr. Hook drove his gray back out of the yard.

Polly Ann drew a deep breath.

"We got just about enough left over for our supper," she said. "We'll milk, and eat, and go to bed. It's been a long day. A wonderful day, though. I never thought to see so good a barn standing here."

But when they had milked, Tom said he had to grease the wheels on the spring wagon. Polly Ann stared at him.

"Why tonight?" she asked. "After all there's been to do."

"I'll tell you when we've ate supper," Tom said.

They were sitting at the kitchen table when he came in, to find four sandwiches on his plate. He couldn't see any more, but Polly Ann said they had had theirs and if anyone was still hungry there was bread and some meat left in the pantry. He ate and took a cup of coffee. All the pies were used up.

He looked from his mother's face to his twin sisters.

"I want to go up to the Breen place tonight," he said.

"*Tonight!*" Polly Ann exclaimed. "*That's* why you greased the wagon wheels?"

He nodded. Ellie and Cissie-Mae just looked bewildered. Polly Ann explained to them that Tom thought he had figured out where Bert and Mrs. Breen had kept their money and she was going to go with him to look for it.

"But I don't see why tonight," she protested. "When we are practically wore out."

"That's why," he answered. "The Flanchers were here nosing around. Yantis begun asking Ox and Mr. Massey why we hadn't brought down the floor for the stable. Yantis may get a notion why I left it. But he wouldn't think of our going up there tonight any more than you did."

He paused a minute.

"It ought to be a good night for us to go. Moon's already set. We won't get more than starlight. And it looks as if it might cloud over too. You think you'd feel able to come with me?" he asked. "After all the work you've been doing all day?"

"Yes, I will," Polly Ann said. "You couldn't keep me from going, no matter if you tried. Besides, you wouldn't ever find your way in from the Irish Settlement road by yourself."

"Then we'll go," Tom said. "We'll wait until half past six, to let it get a little darker."

♦ ♦ ♦

Twilight was beginning to give way to darkness as they topped the long slope up to the canal. He turned Drew to the left, onto the towpath, and glanced at his mother. He could see her profile against the last streak of light along the top of Tug Hill, but only as a silhouette. She had on a thick sweater with a collar that rolled up around her neck under her small, determined chin. He was glad she was coming with him.

Cissie-Mae and Ellie had come out of the house to see them off. He had told them that if anybody came asking for him and Polly Ann they were to say she had been taken sick and he was driving her up to Boonville to see the doctor. No telling when they'd be home. Tom could have hung one of the lanterns he had brought on the dashboard hook, but the light might be seen from a canalside farm, and he didn't want people speculating who might be traveling the towpath that night.

Now he looked back down the valley. It was too dark to see the road from Port Leyden. No lights shone in all the valley except the windows on the Quarry place, and a hundred feet farther along a fold in the ground shut them away. From then on, the wagon moved through the dark with only the reflections of a few early stars on the water of the canal beside the towpath to mark their course. Once, the clank of a cowbell told them a pasture was nearby, and a little later they heard a cow breathe out a heavy sigh, as if she carried the world's sorrow.

Drew paid no attention to such sounds. He plodded on at

his own pace, halfway between a trot and a walk, and Tom let him have his head. The old horse had always been clever at finding his way along a road in the dark.

They made very little sound. The fellies of the wheels hardly whispered as they tracked along the double path beaten by the canal teams. It came as a shock when the thump of Drew's hoofs and the grating of the wheels over sandy gravel echoed suddenly from planking overhead. They had not seen the shadow of the bridge ahead of them. Now for a moment the stars were blotted out. Then they left the bridge behind and were again moving in almost total silence.

There were three more bridges to pass under before they reached the one that carried the Dutch Hill road down into Forestport. The first of these, at Hawkinsville, was the only one that troubled Tom. Unlike the first bridge, it showed up well ahead as they approached, its white timbers picked out against the sky by the dim glow from the village windows on the hill below it. Anyone crossing it was bound to see the spring wagon coming along underneath on the towpath. It all depended on luck; but luck was with them, and not a rig passed over. Drew hauled the wagon underneath and out on the other side. They passed the village without hearing anything at all, not even a dog's bark.

There was small chance of their meeting a canalboat. Boaters didn't like navigating the winding stretch from Forestport to Boonville, with its four-mile current, at night. After Hawkinsville, he and Polly Ann and Drew ought to have the towpath all to themselves. They met no one, and the only lights they saw came from the windows of two small houses, about a quarter mile apart, where the Barton brothers lived.

Both the Bartons were over seventy. They lived by themselves, never having worked up enough nerve to get married. They never spoke to each other, either. But at the same time neither one of them had thought of moving somewhere else.

Tom got to thinking how queer some men could get to be. Now the Flanchers had none of them married, but they lived together in the same house, and they made a lot of trouble for other people. But the Bartons never made trouble for anybody else, beyond one brother telling stories about the other one's meanness.

A heavy mist was lifting off the water. It thickened and kept rising as they went on. By the time they reached Forestport about an hour later, it had risen high enough to blot out the towpath and canal.

They crept ahead in a silence broken only by the sound of the river rapids forty feet below and occasional anxious snorts from the old horse. He seemed to push his way into the mist, going cautious and very slow, his forefeet feeling for the towpath. Tom felt they must be getting close to the Dutch Hill bridge. He put a little pressure on the left rein to warn Drew to look for the turn off the towpath down to the river. The horse seemed able to make it out in some way a human would not comprehend. The wagon pitched downhill, and they went on a step at a time with the mist much heavier against their faces, carrying the cold of river water. Suddenly the wheels rumbled out onto bridge planking. They heard the rush of water underneath. Then the road sloped up and presently the mist began to thin out.

They were moving along a street with houses on each side. Beyond the lighted windows they could see people: three old men sat in front of a stove in a harness shop, which Polly Ann said was Mr. Utley's; in the next house a woman and a small girl were clearing up supper plates. They passed a couple of saloons and a church with a house beside it. Inside a man in a black cassock was talking to a woman who appeared to be crying. After that there was another house standing separate, and then they were in open country, with the mist behind them.

"The road forks a piece ahead," Polly Ann said. "The one to the left goes down to the Armond place, but we take the one straight ahead. It's the Irish Settlement road."

It began with a steep hill. At times the wheels grated on gravel and then bumped with the roughness of the road. Drew heaved against the tugs, uttering grunts of self-pity, but eventually the road leveled off and though they were traveling through woodland, Tom judged they had reached the beginning of the sand-flat country. They passed house lights here and there. As near as he could make out, the houses were mere shanties, all of them one-story, with one or two rooms, built close to the road. Even though there were quite a lot of them, it seemed a lonely place. On the damp, still night air, he could smell poorly tended privies. It wasn't the kind of place he would ever want to live in.

Polly Ann said, "There were a lot of Irish people came over and worked digging the canal. When it was finished they didn't want to go back to the city, so they settled up here. They get what work they can and hunt and fish. I guess they are as poor as us Hannaberrys used to be."

Her saying that made Tom realize that in her mind the Dolan family was better off now. They had the frame of a good barn standing on their place. The determination to get the roof and siding on came back to him again. He slapped the reins on Drew's rump, persuading the old horse into a shuffling trot. The road cleared the settlement and went on across a natural meadow. The sky was speckled bright with stars, framed by the outlines of trees on either side. He could dimly make out the wheel tracks leading on with the path beaten by a single horse between them.

"There's nobody but Nelson Farr uses it," Polly Ann said.

Tom had heard about Farr, a thin, middle-aged, silent man who lived by himself in a weathered house above Wingert's pond. He got paid wages by the Wingerts and the Kehoes for keeping other people from poaching their trout ponds, one above the other, on Crystal Creek. Lower down, Crystal Creek ran into the Armond pond and past their buildings into the Black River; and it was said Farr would take the young Wingerts and Kehoes fishing down it and even fish the Armond pond at night. Parker Munsey had gone up after them more than once, but he had never got close to Farr and the boys. It seemed queer, Tom thought, how wealthy people tried to fish each other's property; same as stealing, some people said. You expected it of poor folks like the Hannaberrys, but not of such as Wingerts and Kehoes.

In the fall Nelson Farr took parties out shooting, first for birds and later on for deer. He always had at least one bird dog living with him in his house, and a hound for running deer. It was the hound, mainly, Tom had on his mind now. The dog slept outside in an old kerosene barrel, Polly Ann said, and if he noticed the wagon going by he would bark. He had a voice, running deer, you could hear half across the township.

Polly Ann said in a low voice, "Nob used to come here once

in a while to fetch Farr whiskey. The hound was a pup then, but he might recognize Drew if he smells him, so long as he's not roused."

◆ ◆ ◆

A faint stir of air came out of the southwest, moving from the house towards the road. They went along with no more sound than the faint plop of Drew's hoofs on the dusty track. Imperceptibly the roof of Farr's house took shape against the stars. Then they could see the corner of one wall against a yellow glow so dim it hardly showed. Farr's kitchen window faced out towards the pond and the lamplight showed he must still be up. As they moved softly along, the glow vanished, and with it the shape of the house. They heard the faint clink of the hound's chain and a low whimpering whine. Whether he had heard them or caught their scent there was no way of knowing. But they were now by and the flat land that marked the end of the Breen place began to open out ahead. The track turned right for fifty feet and then left.

"That's the corner of Armond's land," Polly Ann said. "There used to be good blackberries in there."

What made her think of blackberries now was more than Tom could figure out. He was trying to get his bearings. He thought that Breen's Hill ought to show up just ahead, but he couldn't make it out. And he knew they would have to get across Cold Brook yet, to reach the barn.

He felt Polly Ann's hand on his arm.

"We better get down and lead Drew."

She pointed to a line of scattered trees barely visible against the stars.

82

"We want to get near them, Tom. There's a farm track goes along them to Cold Brook. That's where the ford is."

They led Drew ahead. He didn't like it much now he was off the road, poor as it had been, but as they were walking beside him he made no objection, and he turned instinctively as his hoofs felt the track she had mentioned, before they themselves were aware of it. They followed it towards the brook until the land began to slope down.

"This ought to be Cold Brook," Polly Ann said just above a whisper; and sure enough, now they were stopped Tom could hear the gurgle of moving water.

He looked around for something to tie Drew to. The old horse wouldn't wander far, but Tom didn't want him moving at all if it could be helped. A little way off a dark shadow stood on the land about eight feet high. It was a young white pine. He led Drew over to it and tied him to it with a hitching rope. His silhouette and that of the pine would make one shape, supposing anybody would be able to see that far from where the house was. Then he felt in the wagon for one of the lanterns he had brought and his pinch bar. He didn't intend to light the lantern unless he had to.

"I'm going over there now," he said in a low voice. "You stay here, Ma."

"I will not. I'm coming with you, Tom."

Her voice was so determined it was as good as seeing her cocked chin and set jaw. When she sounded that way, there wasn't much use trying to change her mind.

The wheel tracks deepened as they generally did on each bank at a brook crossing and Tom felt his way down, trying to keep between them. When he stepped into the water, it was so cold he was glad he hadn't put off coming until the black part of November. His legs were numbed from the knee down, even though the brook was less than eight feet across. He heard Polly Ann draw her breath sharply just behind him. Then they were both going up the other bank.

The floor of the barn was no more than two hundred feet ahead. They approached it slowly, finding their way by the wagon track until what was left of the Breen house showed up on their left, a black and gloomy smudge against the stars. There was no light, no sign of a person anywhere, but they stood still together, straining to hear any sound. Behind them a barred owl started hooting in the Armond woods. The bird repeated itself twice and then fell silent. Presently from the big swamp east of the Breen place, another answered. Then they began a dialogue, punctuated by silences of varying lengths as if what each said in turn was of variable importance.

Listening, Tom fell into a sort of trance until Polly Ann took his arm.

"Just two fool birds calling," she said. "We hadn't ought to waste more time."

Tom gave himself a shake. He didn't know what had got into him, but his head came clear. He led the way to where the barn had stood and all at once they felt the floor timbers of the cow run under their feet.

Tom set the lantern down close to where the sill had been.

"I don't want to light it unless I've got to," he said quietly. "Anyways until I've found where the money is. If it's there."

"It's there, Tom," Polly Ann said, almost in a murmur. "Don't you doubt it."

But now that he was about really to look for it all his confidence seemed to have gone. His idea had been that Bert Breen would not have had his loose flooring too near his box of sand and chaff, maybe halfway down the length of the barn. But it seemed best to begin at one end and work straight on until he did or didn't find something loose. He was sure that they wouldn't be right inside the door, but he began there anyway.

He was right. All the timbers were spiked solid to the three stringers underneath them. He kept on giving one after another a pry with his pinch bar until he was well past where the box was. They continued to be spiked fast all the way past the middle and a cold doubt about his being dead wrong in his ideas took hold of his mind. Then he thought maybe the natural place to look would have been the far end. He was tempted to go down and try. But it seemed better to keep on the way he was going. If the money wasn't at the far end, he'd have wasted that much more time.

He heard the sound of Polly Ann's feet moving quietly down the run behind him. She said, very softly, "Tom."

But he had the pinch bar prying against the end of the next timber, and it lifted.

"What is it, Ma?"

"The owls have stopped hollering," she said. "If they *was* owls."

"They're owls all right, Ma. They've just said everything they had to say."

"Perhaps. But the second one has flew up out of the swamp and now he's near the road, opposite us," she said. "He was the one quit first."

"Well, I've got a loose piece here," Tom said. "I better try the next."

He lifted the loose timber out and laid it to one side. He took hold of the next one with his hand, and it was loose also. Then the next and a fourth. He put them down in order so he could put them back the way they'd been. Polly Ann was kneeling at the edge of the uncovered space.

"Tom," she whispered. "They made a hole here, and there's a couple of trunks in it."

He touched her arm and felt her trembling. Or maybe it was himself. He listened against the dark, but heard only the crickets.

He had to struggle to control his voice, even to whisper. "Are they heavy, Ma?"

She tugged. "Yes. Kind of. But I guess we can carry them all right."

He moved over to kneel beside her and felt for the first trunk. It was small, maybe three feet by two on top, he judged. It oughtn't to be too heavy.

He got a grip on the handles and heaved it up. It was a good deal heavier than he'd expected, but he got it out without much trouble. The second was a bit smaller but seemed to weigh even more. He heaved it out also.

"We've got to get them over to the wagon," he said.

She whispered, "Yes."

Each of them took hold of a handle of the second trunk and started back towards Cold Brook. It was harder to make their way in the dark carrying the trunk. The weight interfered with their balance and it was necessary to move very slowly. They made a good deal more noise, also, crossing the brook. But finally they got the trunk up the far bank and located Drew and the spring wagon and heaved the trunk onto the wagon bed.

Polly Ann was breathing quite hard, but she wouldn't hear of resting and they went straight back for the other trunk. Its larger size made it clumsier to handle, but it wasn't quite so heavy, and made the second trip seem easier. They got it onto the wagon with no trouble and Tom said, "I want you to take Drew back to the corner of the Armond land. If anybody shows up they won't see you that far off, and if there's any kind of a commotion here you better start going home. I'll walk back."

"What do you aim to do, Tom?"

"I want to get those floor timbers back where they were," he told her. "And scatter some of that sand and chaft over them."

"All right. I'll go over to the corner, but I won't start home till you get there too, Tom."

She watched him turn back towards the barn.

"Tom," she said quietly. "Don't forget to bring the lantern."

Tom had forgotten all about it, never having had to use it. He raised his hand, not thinking that she couldn't see him at all. After he crossed the brook, he could hear her taking Drew away across the open land towards Armond's corner.

◆ ◆ ◆

He had no trouble finding the loose timbers and it didn't take long to fit them back in place, even in the dark, for he had laid them down in proper order. He felt his way back then along the flooring to the box where the chaff and sand was, and it was then he realized he hadn't brought anything to carry it in. He tried to remember if there was an old shovel lying about.

But he couldn't recall having seen any such thing. There would probably be a saucepan or something in the house. But to find one he would have to light his lantern, and he didn't want to do that. He scratched his head, wondering what to do. His hat tilted over his eyes and suddenly it came to him that it would do as well as a saucepan. He set it down in the box, filled it with handfuls of sand, and carried it back to the loose timbers. He would have liked some lantern light now. Scattering sand evenly in the dark wasn't easy. Besides, from having been out in the weather, it was damp. He had to hope that a night's dew would make it appear more natural. But that was only a guess. He went back for another hatful, wondering how long they had spent at Breen's. Too long, he thought. And all at once he felt a trickle of sweat between his shoulders run down to the small of his back. He went back to the loose timbers and scattered the second hatful as well as he could.

He was going to get a third, but before he reached the box a light appeared on the road. It came along smoothly, so he knew it was on a wagon. A lantern carried by hand always has a kind of bob to it. Whoever it was could be coming only to Breen's.

There wasn't time for any more sand. He felt around for his own lantern, which he had put in one corner of the box of sand, and picked it up. It was time to vamoose. He went down to Cold Brook and waded through just as the wagon lantern turned the corner to come into the Breen place. He moved up the bank to where they had left the wagon and stood close beside the pine tree. He could see the wagon come up to the barn floor. A man got down; then two more. To his mind they couldn't be anybody but Flanchers.

He drew back behind the pine and when it was between him and the men, set off across the open land to find Drew and Polly Ann. He kept himself from hurrying. Rapid motion could attract attention no matter how dark it was. He moved evenly and slowly, making as little noise and disturbance as he knew how, his legs brushing easily through blueberry bushes. And in about five minutes he was nearing the corner of Armond's back line.

With the woods and underbrush beyond, Tom could see absolutely nothing of the wagon or Polly Ann, but presently he heard Drew blowing deep, soft breaths in his direction and when he reached out his hand it met the felly of a rear wheel.

"Ma," he said quietly. "It's me."

"I know," she said. "Drew heard you first and then I did. Coming so quiet I knowed it was you."

He said, "There's three men back at the barn. It's the Flanchers, probably. I'm going to lead Drew until we get around the bend and up past Farr's."

He felt his way along the wagon and stroked Drew's shoulder. The old horse blubbered his lips on the back of Tom's hand as he reached for the chin strap, and the wagon started forward with hardly a sound. Tom was glad, now, he had greased the wheels.

They moved on, feeling for the track, turned the corner, and in a minute or two were behind Farr's house once more. Tom couldn't see any light from the kitchen window this time. The hound was quiet, too. There was no sound of his chain. Tom continued leading Drew, though, till they reached the foot of Kehoe's pond and crossed the bridge over Crystal Creek. He felt it was safe to stop for a few minutes then, and he went back along the wagon, telling Polly Ann to hold the lines.

"I want to tie those trunks down," he told her.

He had brought a length of light rope which he passed through the trunk handles, securing the ends to rings on the sides of the wagon bed. And then at last he lit a lantern.

"You think it's safe going with a light?" Polly Ann asked.

"I want to make better time," he said. He hung the lantern on the dashboard hook and for a minute it blinded them, as if the night had suddenly become a room with solid walls around them. But in a moment their eyes became accustomed to the light and then they could see a bit of the road reaching forward from Drew's front hoofs. Drew plainly liked the change, for he started ahead without a word from Tom or a hitch of the lines. They could see each other, too.

"Why don't you put your hat on?" Polly Ann asked him.

"I used it to carry sand and chaff in," he told her. "I shook it, but there's still some left in it."

She gave a sniff. "I'd have thought a boy your age would have sense to turn his hat inside out if he was going to put dirt into it."

"I know, Ma," he said sheepishly. "But there wasn't anything else to carry it in, and I wanted to get away from there."

"Yes," she said, and he could see she was smiling a little. Then she asked what was in both their minds. "Why do you suppose those Flanchers came up to Breen's tonight, Tom?"

"I don't know. I thought they'd started back home. They'd think after the raising we was too tired to do anything but go to bed."

"Maybe they came back just to check up. And when they saw the spring wagon and Drew was gone, they asked the girls."

"We told them to say I'd taken you to the doctor," Tom said.

Polly Ann nodded. "But they didn't believe it. They came up to Breen's instead. Likely, when they don't find anything, they'll go back to our place."

"I was thinking that too," Tom said. "I don't think we should take the money back home."

Polly Ann agreed. "But where could we take it?"

"I was wondering if Billy-Bob Baxter would be up still."

"I don't know," Polly Ann said. "But I've heard he sits up most of the night sometimes."

They were passing through the Irish Settlement. There were no lights at all now, except their own traveling the edge of the road as Drew pulled the wagon in a steady trot. Once a door opened — they could hear the hinge squeak — but whoever looked out didn't have anything to say. Then they were rolling down the steep hill and five minutes later, passing through Forestport.

There were lights in the saloons and Utley's harness shop, but the rest of the buildings were dark. Tom caught sight of a wall clock through the saloon window; he thought it said half past eleven.

"It'll be way past midnight when we get to Boonville," he said.

"Never mind," Polly Ann said. "We'll go to Mr. Baxter's, and if it shows no lights, we'll knock until he comes to his door."

Tom had to agree, for he couldn't think of anything else for them to do.

The mist had left the river. After they crossed the bridge he turned Drew into the Dutch Hill road, and they went up the steep pitch to the canal. They got past the house beside the towpath before anybody came out. But a man yelled after them, wanting to know where they thought they were going this late.

Tom didn't answer. He hoped they had got far enough away so they could not be recognized.

◆ ◆ ◆

Misgivings seized Tom as Drew turned the corner into Leyden Street, his hoofs thumping a loud tattoo on the packed dry dirt. Boonville had gone to bed. The only lighted window they had seen since coming off the towpath opposite the depot was in the front of Dr. Grover's house, no doubt left on for his return from some protracted childbirth on a back farm.

Calling on anybody so late at night didn't seem a proper thing to do, but as they rolled up the street he was reassured to see a light reach out towards the street from a window of the lawyer's little house. Billy-Bob Baxter was undoubtedly still up, working his mind over whatever case he had in hand at the moment. Tom turned Drew into the drive beside the house, so that the wagon was hardly noticeable from the street, and gave Polly Ann the lines to hold while he went up on the front porch and knocked gently on a pane of the office window. He couldn't see Billy-Bob from where he stood, but he heard the scrape of his desk chair being shoved back and presently the lawyer came into view, looking just the way he had before in his worn, shiny jacket and a trail of cigar ash down his waist-coat. He had taken his watch from its pocket and now he was putting it back. When he saw Tom standing outside the window, he nodded and a moment later opened the front door.

"Well, Tom," he said, "must be something on your mind to bring you here this late. I heard you had a barn raising on your place today."

Tom said, yes, they had had one.

"Should have thought that would be enough for one day, even for a strapper like you. But come in and tell me what you want."

Tom didn't go in. He told how he and Polly Ann had decided to go up to the Breen place, and why. And then how the Flanchers had showed up. They'd been lucky to get away.

Billy-Bob looked at him a minute.

"You mean you found something, Tom?"

Tom told him. "Two trunks, not big ones."

"With money into them?"

"We didn't want to stop to look."

"You've got them outside in the wagon? Where anybody can see them?"

"Yes. But it's around the side of the house and Ma's sitting in it."

"Well," Billy-Bob said, almost fussily. "We can't have them out there. You go and lead your horse around to the back and we'll bring the trunks and Polly Ann in through the kitchen. Then put your horse in my barn and come inside yourself."

It took only a few minutes to get the trunks into the kitchen, where Billy-Bob made a jerky little bow towards Polly Ann and said he remembered her when she was no bigger than a

93

shaving, "but mighty pretty you were. And still are, Mrs. Dolan."

Tom went out to lead Drew into the barn. Billy-Bob no longer kept a horse. Tom found some oats in a bin, but they smelled stale and sour, so the old horse would have to go hungry until he got home. Tom told him he was sorry and left him standing there, probably philosophizing on the unreasonableness of people.

Polly Ann and Billy-Bob had moved the trunks into his office and the shades had been pulled down over the windows.

"Let's get them up on my desk," Billy-Bob said.

They showed they had been in the ground. There was some mildew on the leather sides, but they still looked sturdy and the smaller one had wood slats reinforcing it. Both of them were locked.

"Seems a shame to break them," said the lawyer. He pulled open a drawer in his desk and took out a flat box filled with keys. "Ought to be something in this lot to open them up. Here. Try that one, Tom."

It didn't fit the lock of the first trunk at all. It entered the keyhole of the second lock, but Tom couldn't turn it.

"Put it to the side," Billy-Bob said, "and try this one."

None of the first eight keys worked. But with the ninth, Tom gave a twist and saw the hasp move a bit. He got out his jacknife and pried with the blade and the hasp came free. But he hesitated about lifting the lid.

"Open her up," Billy-Bob said impatiently.

Tom obeyed. A piece of muslin cloth covered the top and Polly Ann lifted it. Underneath were bundles and bundles of money, each tied with a fine string. Polly Ann's face flushed scarlet, right to her hair, and then turned white, and Tom remembered what she had said about herself and Mr. Hook, and being poor. And then with a sinking feeling he wondered whether they would be entitled to keep any of it.

Billy-Bob Baxter broke the silence with a kind of chortling noise in the back of his nose and said, "Looks like there's quite a pile of money there, if old Bert Breen didn't keep his underwear underneath it."

Tom lifted out a bundle It seemed to be all ten-dollar bills.

Polly Ann said, "I think we ought to open up the other trunk and then count all the money at once."

"I agree," Billy-Bob said. So they went to trying keys, and the eighteenth or twentieth fitted the second trunk. When Tom heaved up the lid, they saw it was loaded full of money like the first one.

"Well," Billy-Bob said, "let's start counting it."

He gave Polly Ann and Tom each a pad and pencil, telling them to put down the total of each bundle, and put the figure on a strip of paper to go under the string when they tied the money up again. That way none of the bundles could get counted a second time. Then they would put all the totals together and find out how much money the whole lot amounted to.

It took them quite a while. The square black clock with a brass horse on top of it, that stood on the shelf behind the small chunk stove, struck one and then it struck one again for the half hour before they had finished counting. The piles of counted bundles mounted up more than you would have thought from seeing them inside the two trunks. Billy-Bob drew a long breath and got out a big pad of yellow paper and asked Polly

Ann to read off the totals of her bundles, putting each one aside as she read it. He jotted down the figures in a column. Then Tom read off the figures for his bundles, and Billy-Bob listed them in a second column. Finally he read off his own pile and made a third column.

After that he added up each column in turn, letting out a soft hissing sound between his teeth. When he was done, he added the three figures, still hissing, and for a long minute he just sat there looking at the complete total while Tom and Polly Ann sat wordlessly watching.

"Well, Tom. By this count you're eight thousand seven hundred seventy-nine dollars richer than you were yesterday when you and Polly Ann went up to Bert Breen's. That doesn't include the loose silver in the bottom of the little trunk, but I don't expect it will amount to any big amount more. The question is, what are you going to do with it?"

Tom couldn't find words to answer. In all the thinking he had done about Breen's money, he hadn't thought of what it might amount to. If he had, he would never have thought of it coming to anything as big as half that amount. He just didn't know how to answer Billy-Bob.

"Well," the lawyer said. "You can't keep it around here. I'm not going to sit on what will come to maybe nine thousand dollars cash money in my house. You've got to get it into the bank."

"I wouldn't want to take it home," Tom answered. "On account of Yantis Flancher."

"I agree. I'll keep it here for tonight. But tomorrow I'll take it down to the bank. I'll hire a rig from Joe Hemphill and aim to deliver it there at nine o'clock, sharp. You be there, too."

He chuckled suddenly. "It's going to be worth the whole amount to see Oscar Lambert's face. We won't tell him it's Bert Breen's money. We'll just tell him you had a cash inheritance, Tom. He'll guess. No doubt about it. But he won't bring himself to ask."

"Couldn't we say Tom inherited it from his Great-Uncle Phister?" Polly Ann asked. "That's how I come to name him Tom. Uncle Phister was wealthy. He kept his own carriage, with a hired coachman, too."

"No," Billy-Bob said. "The less lies you tell about something like this, the better. As a matter of fact we won't say it was an inheritance at all. We'll just say Tom came into money." He looked from one to the other with his thin smile. "The less talk about it there is, the better. Now, I suggest we put the money back in the trunks and Tom locks them. And he keeps the keys. You'll unlock them tomorrow in front of Oscar Lambert and he and his teller will have to count it all over again. They can count the silver at the same time. After that, Tom, we can come back here and discuss what you're going to do with it."

They packed it back in the trunks. Tom locked them and put the keys in his pocket and helped Billy-Bob carry the trunks into a closet off the office, the door of which Billy-Bob locked also. Then Tom and Polly Ann went out, got Drew out of the barn, and started home. They hardly had a word to say all the way, except that Polly Ann drew a deep breath after they crossed Fisk Bridge and said, "Oh Tom, it's going to be so different for us now!"

A Narrow Escape

Will James

I was riding along one day whistling a tune, my horse was behaving fine and all was hunkydory and peaceful. Ahead a ways I'd noticed a narrow washout and I kept on a riding. I'd rode over many a one of them, and nothing was there to warn me that I should go around this perticular one.

My horse cleared the opening and I was still a whistling, then, of a sudden my whistling stopped short as I felt the earth go out from under my horse's feet, . . . the next thing I know I was in the bottom of a ten-foot washout and underneath twelve hundred pounds of horseflesh.

I was pinned there to stay, and lucky I thought afterward that my whole body wasn't underneath that horse. It could of just as well been that way, only past experiences with horses had saved me and natural instinct had made me try to stay on top of the horse whether he was upside down or right side up. As it was, I was kind of on the side of him, my head was along his neck and only my left hip and leg felt the pinch of the weight.

The washout was only about three feet wide, at the bottom,

just enough room for me and that horse to get wedged in nice. The old pony was fighting and bellering and kicking big hunks of dirt down on top of us. I was kinda worried that he might undermine the bank of the washout and have it cave in on us and bury us alive so I grabbed his head and hugged it toward me thinking that would quiet him down and keep him from tearing things up so much. I figgered that if there'd be any squeezing done it would be on the other side, for as it was I sure had no room to spare.

Well, he fought on for quite a spell, then he laid still for a while. If that horse had been good and gentle I could of maybe got him to lay still long enough so I could try and dig myself out with my hands, but just as soon as I'd move to try anything like that he'd let out a snort that sounded mighty loud in that perticular place and go to fighting again.

His hoofs would start flying and tearing things up and what little dirt I'd scraped away with my fingers would be replaced with a few hundred pounds of the side of the washout. I was having a mighty hard time keeping my head clear and out in the air and the dirt kept accumulating and piling up on top of us till there was nothing but part of the horse's legs, still a going, and our heads sticking out.

Then it comes to me that if that horse keeps on a kicking and bringing down more dirt he'd soon be in a fix where his legs would be all buried and he'd have to be still, but I was sure worried about a big hunk of overhanging dirt he might loosen up while doing that. It looked like it weighed at least five tons and I didn't want to think of it dropping down on us.

There was one way where I could win out, and that was to dig for my six-shooter which it was lucky was on my right hip and possible to get at. With that six-gun I could shoot the horse, there'd be no more dirt coming down and I could easy enough dig myself out with the same gun, and I could take my time about it too.

That was one way and the best one, but I sure didn't want to shoot that horse and decided I wouldn't till I just had to to save him from suffering. Shooting a horse wasn't appealing to me even in the fix I was in. I would of saved my carcass for sure but I was finding more pleasure in looking for other ways out than just that one.

I kept my eye on the hunk of dirt above my head, and while the pony by me would have another fit once in a while and small piles of dirt would keep a coming down I was finding my breathing capacity getting smaller and smaller. My body was beginning to feel numb from my chest on down and I felt that the only part of me that was living was from my chest on up.

I thought of the boys I started out from camp with that morning and wondered *when* they'd miss me and start looking for me, and then once again I thought of my six-gun. If I could get it out and fire a shot once in a while some of 'em would maybe hear.

I'd been digging pretty steady and with just the idea of keeping my right arm and head clear. I knowed that I couldn't get away even if all the dirt was off — the horse was on me and holding me down, but from then on I wanted my gun and I sure went to work for it.

It took me a good hour's time to get it out and my gloves was wore to a frazzle, but I finally managed it, and soon as I shook the dirt out of the barrel I held it straight up and fired.

The shot echoed along the washout and sounded like it could be heard for many miles. I waited and listened for an answer and then I noticed where the sun was. It was slanting in where me and my pony was getting buried alive and it was making things all the hotter down there.

By it I figgered it was along about noon, all the boys excepting me would be back to camp from the first "circle" and wouldn't be starting out again for a while. I was about ten miles from camp and when they would start out again I knowed they'd go another direction as all the cattle in the country I was at was run in that morning. The shot I fired had been for nothing.

Riders was often late getting in with cattle and I knowed they hadn't thought anything had happened to me as yet. I also knowed they wouldn't think anything was wrong till that evening when they gathered in to eat, and till then I thought was an ungodly long time to wait.

And what was more, how was they going to find me if they did start looking. I was sure well hid and they'd have to pretty near know the exact spot where I was located, I could make a noise with my gun of course. . . . All them thoughts was mighty cheerful thoughts not to have, but I couldn't dodge 'em. If only that big ton of dirt above my head hadn't been so threatening things would of been easier, but there it was as big as death and I couldn't take my eyes from it.

Finally the sun left us. It was going on west to its setting point and left me still doing some tall thinking. The big horse alongside of me was quiet for good — the dirt had piled up on top of him till his toes disappeared and he *had* to be still. But his breathing wasn't very good to listen to so close to my head, and I didn't find it at all inspiring as to ways and means of getting out of there.

Clods of dirt would still keep a falling off and on but there was signs of 'em quitting since the horse had got quiet. It was too late for me to try to dig out though, but I was still at it and at the same time watching that I didn't tickle or jar the side of the bank that held the all-powerful heavy piece of earth.

As I worked and clawed at the dirt and wished for badger claws instead of bleeding fingers I found that my resting spells was coming oftener and stayed longer. It was just as the sun was going down and when I'd took an *unusual* long rest that I realized I was holding something in my hand that I'd grabbed a hold of when I was ready to quit. It was a clump of rabbit brush that'd fell in from the top with the dirt that'd got loosened — more of it was a hanging up there.

My hand was on my chest as I studied where that piece of brush had come from. I felt a chill run up and down my backbone as I realized that it'd come from no other place than the big hunk of overhanging dirt. *It was loosening up.*

The thought of that near had me moving, my hand closed in on my shirt just for something to grab a hold of, and as I did that I felt something breaking in my shirt pocket. It was matches.

I held my hand there for a while and done some thinking. I noticed the clump of rabbit brush my hand was still holding and then I looked up ten feet above to where there was lots of the same brush hanging over the edge.

I couldn't think so very fast along about then and I only realized it was dark when I lit a match ands it throwed a light, but the rest of the programme didn't need no thinking — everything was in front of me to follow and that's what I did.

I held the match under the piece of rabbit brush I had and it took holt and flamed like that kind of brush does. When I thought the flame was strong enough to stand a little breeze I heaved it as best I could up toward the other brush ten feet above me.

The first attempt wasn't much good, the little piece of brush came back on me, singed me a little and then died. I tried it again and finally landed it up amongst the brush along the top of the bank. Then I held my breath.

A little flame shot up and throwed a light on the opposite side of the washout. I watched that and seen where the flame seemed to gradually die down. "If that fire don't start," I says out loud, "I'm just as good as done for," which was the truth.

But it did start, slow and aggravating but sure, and pretty soon it gets lit up above, and I can see the sparks fly and some of 'em are falling down on me and the horse but it was sure good to see that light and hear that brush a roaring in flame. I knowed what rabbit brush would do once it got started to burning. I knowed it'd spread and throw a mighty good light for as long as any of that kind of brush was around. And if I remembered right, that kind of brush was plenty thick along that wash for a good mile or so.

From then on instead of digging I put my efforts to waiting and that was getting to be some painful too, but my hopes had went up a lot since I got such a good signal fire started. I felt sure somebody would ride up and look for me soon, and sure enough, after a while I hear somebody holler, my six-shooter barks out an answer and then I thinks, . . . what if somebody should ride upon that piece of country that's hanging over me and just waiting for some little weight to start it down.

The thought of that sure got my lungs to working. . . . "Stay back," I hollered, "stay back."

"Where are you, Bill?" somebody asks.

"In the bottom of the washout," I answers, "but don't come near the edge of where I'm at or it'll cave in — get in from some other place."

I didn't have to tell them to hurry, they was doing that a plenty and pretty soon half a dozen riders was digging me out with running irons, six-shooters, and everything they could get hold of that'd scatter the dirt. The horse was lifted off of me and I was pulled out to where I could work my legs and get the blood to circulating in 'em.

It took four saddle horses to pull my horse out and straighten him up to stand, and by the time I got through telling the boys what happened, how it happened and all, I felt half-ways strong enough to stand up again. With the help of one of the boys I walked over to investigate the hunk of earth that'd been hanging over me and threatening all that long day. There was a crack in the ground and back of it which showed how ready it was to fall. I stuck my boot heel in that crack and shoved a little, and about that time I was pulled away.

The earth seemed to go out from under us as that hunk left, a big cloud of dust went up, and when we looked again the washout was near filled to the top.

El Enano

Charles J. Finger

Everyone disliked El Enano who lived in the forest, because
he always lay hidden in dark places, and when woodmen
passed he jumped out on them and beat them and took their
dinners from them. He was a squat creature, yellow of skin
and snag-toothed and his legs were crooked, his arms were
crooked, and his face was crooked. There were times when he
went about on all fours and then he looked like a great spider,
for he had scraggy whiskers that hung to the ground and
looked like legs. At other times he had the mood to make himself very small like a little child, and then he was most horrible
to see, for his skin was wrinkled and his whiskers hung about
him like a ragged garment.

Yet all of that the people might have forgiven and he might
have been put up with, were it not for some worse tricks. What
was most disliked was his trick of walking softly about a house
in the night-time while the people were inside, suspecting nothing, perhaps singing and talking. Seeing them thus, El Enano
would hide in the shadows until someone went for water to the
spring, then out he would leap, clinging fast to the hair of the

105

boy or man and beating, biting, scratching the while. Being released, the tortured one would of course run to reach the house, but El Enano would hop on one leg behind, terribly fast, and catch his victim again just as a hand was almost laid on the door latch. Nor could an alarm be raised, because El Enano cast a spell of silence, so that, try as one would, neither word nor shout would come.

Then there was his other evil trick of hiding close to the ground and reaching out a long and elastic arm to catch boy or girl by the ankle. But that was not worse than his habit of making a noise like hail or rain, hearing which the people in the house would get up to close a window, and there, looking at them from the dark but quite close to their faces, would be the grinning Enano holding in his hands his whiskers that looked like a frightening curtain, his eyes red and shining like rubies. That was very unpleasant indeed, especially when a person was alone in the house. Nor was it much better when he left the window, for he would hop and skip about the house yard for hours, screaming and howling and throwing sticks and stones. So, wherever he was there was chill horror.

One day, a good old woman who lived alone went with her basket to gather berries. El Enano saw her and at once made himself into a little creature no larger than a baby and stretched himself on a bed of bright moss between two trees leafless and ugly. He pretended to be asleep, though he whimpered a little as a child does when it has a bad dream.

The good old woman was short-sighted but her ears were quick, and hearing the soft whimper she found the creature and took it in her arms. To do that bent her sadly, for Enano when small was the same weight as when his full size.

"Oh, poor thing," she said. "Someone has lost a baby. Or perhaps some wild creature has carried the tender thing from its home. So, lest it perish I will take care of it, though to be sure, a heavier baby I never held."

The dame had no children of her own and, though poor, was both willing and glad to share what she had with any needy creature. Gently she took it home and having put dry sticks on the fire she made a bed of light twigs which she covered with a mat of feathers. Then she bustled about, getting bread and milk for supper for the little one, feeling happy at heart because she had rescued the unhappy creature from the dismal forest.

At first she was glad to see the appetite of the homeless thing, for it soon finished the bread and milk and cried for more.

"Bless me! It must be half starved," she said. "It may have my supper." So she took the food she had set out for herself and El Enano swallowed it as quickly as he had swallowed the first bowl. Yet still he cried for more. Off then to the neighbours she went, borrowing milk from this one, bread from that, rice from another, until half the children of the village had to go on short commons that night. The creature devoured all that was brought and still yelled for more and the noise it made was ear-splitting. But as it ate and felt the warmth, it grew and grew.

"Santa Maria!" said the dame. "What wonderful thing is this? Already it is no longer a baby, but a grown child. Almost it might be called ugly, but that, I suppose, is because it was motherless and lost. It is all very sad." Then, because she had thought it ugly she did the more for it, being sorry for her thoughts, though she could not help nor hinder them. As for the creature itself, having eaten all in the house, it gave a grunt or two, turned heavily on its side and went to sleep, snoring terribly.

Next morning matters were worse, for El Enano was stretched out on the floor before the fire, his full size, and seeing the dame he called for food, making so great a noise that the very windows shook and his cries were heard all over the village. So to still him, and there being nothing to eat in the house, the good old woman went out and told her tale to the neighbours, asking their help and advice, and to her house they all went flocking to look at the strange creature. One man, a stout-hearted fellow, told El Enano that it was high time for him to be going, hearing which, the ugly thing shrieked with wicked laughter.

"Well, bring me food," it said, looking at the man with red eyes. "Bring me food, I say, and when I have eaten enough I may leave you. But bring me no child's food, but rather food for six and twenty men. Bring an armadillo roasted and a pig and a large goose and many eggs and the milk of twenty cows. Nor be slow about it, for I must amuse myself while I wait and it may well be that you will not care for the manner of my amusement."

Indeed, there was small likelihood of any one there doing that, for his amusement was in breaking things about the house, the tables and benches, the pots and the ollas, and when he had made sad havoc of the woman's house he started on the house next door, smashing doors and windows, tearing up flowers by the roots, chasing the milk goats and the chickens, and setting dogs to fight. Nor did he cease in his mischief until the meal was set out for him, when he leaped upon it and crammed it down his throat with fearful haste, leaving neither bone nor crumb.

The people of the village stood watching, whispering one to another behind their hands, how they were shocked at all that sight, and when at last the meal was finished, the stouthearted man who had spoken before stepped forward. "Now sir!" said he to El Enano, "seeing that you have eaten enough and more than enough, you will keep your word, going about your business and leaving this poor woman and us in peace. Will you?"

"No. *No*. NO!" roared El Enano, each No being louder than the one before it.

"But you promised," said the man.

What the creature said when answering that made nearly everyone there faint with horror. It said:

"What I promised was that I would leave when I had eaten enough. I did not —"

The bold man interrupted then, saying, "Well, you have eaten enough."

"Ah yes, for one meal," answered the cruel Enano. "But I meant that I would leave when I have eaten enough for always. There is tomorrow and tomorrow night. There is the day after that and the next day and the next day. There are to be weeks of eating and months of eating and years of eating. You are stupid people if you think that I shall ever have eaten enough. So I shall not leave. No. *No*. NO!"

Having said that, the creature laughed in great glee and began to throw such things as he could reach against the walls, and so, many good things were shattered.

Now for three days that kind of thing went on, at the end

of which time the men of the place were at their wits' ends to know what to do, for almost everything eatable in the village had gone down the creature's throat. Sad at heart, seeing what had come to pass, the good old woman went out and sat down to weep by the side of a quiet pool, for it seemed to her to be a hard thing that what she had done in kindness had ended thus, and that the house she had built and loved and kept clean and sweet should be so sadly wrecked and ruined. Her thoughts were broken by the sound of a voice, and turning she saw a silver-gray fox sitting on a rock and looking at her.

"It is well enough to have a good cry," he said, "but it is better to be gay and have a good laugh."

"Ah! Good evening, Señor Zorro," answered the dame, drying her tears. "But who can be gay when a horrible creature is eating everything? Who can be otherwise than sad, seeing the trouble brought on friends?" The last she added, being one of those who are always saddened by the cheerlessness of others.

"You need not tell me," said the fox. "I know everything that has passed," and he put his head a little sideways like a wise young dog and seemed to smile.

"But what is there to do?" asked the dame. "I am in serious case indeed. This alocado says that he will make no stir until he has had enough to eat for all his life; and certainly he makes no stir to go away."

"The trouble is that you give him enough and not too much," said the fox.

"Too much, you say? We have given him too much already, seeing that we have given him all that we have," said the old dame a little angrily.

"Well, what you must do is to give him something that he does not like. Then he will go away," said the fox.

"Easier said than done," answered the old woman with spirit. "Did we but give him something of which he liked not the taste, then he would eat ten times more to take the bad taste away. Señor Zorro, with all your cleverness, you are but a poor adviser."

After that the fox thought a long while before saying anything, then coming close to the old woman and looking up into her face he said:

"Make your mind easy. He shall have enough to eat this very night and all that you have to do is to see that your neighbours do as I say, nor be full of doubt should I do anything that seems to be contrary."

So the good old woman promised to warn her neighbours, knowing well the wisdom of the fox, and together they went to her house, where they found El Enano stretched out on the floor, looking like a great pig, and every minute he gave a great roar. The neighbours were both angry and afraid, for the creature had been very destructive that day. Indeed, he had taken delight in stripping the thatched roofs and had desisted only when the men of the place had promised to double the amount of his meal.

Not five minutes had the fox and the dame been in the house when the men of the place came in with things — with berries and armadillos, eggs and partridges, turkeys and bread and much fish from the lake. At once they set about cooking, while the women commenced to brew a great bowl of knot-grass tea. Soon the food was cooked and El Enano fell to as greedily as ever.

The fox looked at Enano for a while, then said:

"You have a fine appetite, my friend. What will there be for the men and the women and the children and for me to eat?"

"You may have what I leave, and eat it when I end," said El Enano.

"Let us hope then that our appetites will be light," said the fox.

A little later the fox began to act horribly, jumping about the room and whining, and calling the people lazy and inhospitable.

"Think you," he said, "that this is the way to treat a visitor? A pretty thing indeed to serve one and let the other go hungry. Do I get nothing at all to eat? Quick. Bring me potatoes and roast them, or it will be bad for all of you. The mischief I do shall be ten times worse than any done already."

Knowing that some plan was afoot the people ran out of the house and soon came back with potatoes, and the fox showed them how he wanted them roasted on the hearth. So they were placed in the ashes and covered with hot coals and when they were well done the fox told everyone to take a potato, saying that El Enano, who was crunching the bones of the animals he had eaten, would not like them. But all the while the men were eating, the fox ran from one to another whispering things, but quite loud enough for Enano to hear. "Hush!" said he. "Say nothing. El Enano must not know how good they are and when he asks for some, tell him that they are all gone."

"Yes. Yes," said the people, keeping in with the plan. "Do not let Enano know."

By this time El Enano was suspicious and looked from one man to another. "Give me all the potatoes," he said.

"They are all eaten except mine," said the fox, "but you may taste that." So saying he thrust the roasted potato into the hands of Enano and the creature crammed it down its throat at once.

"Ha! It is good," he roared. "Give me more. More. MORE."

"We have no more," said the fox very loud, then, quite softly to those who stood near him, he added, "Say nothing about the potatoes on the hearth," but loudly enough for El Enano to hear, though quite well he knew that there were none.

"Ah! I heard you," roared El Enano. "There are potatoes on the hearth. Give them to me."

"We must let him have them," said the fox, raking the red-hot coals to the front.

"Out of the way," cried El Enano, reaching over the fox and scooping up a double handful of hot coals, believing them to be potatoes. Red hot as they were he swallowed them and in another moment was rolling on the floor, howling with pain as the fire blazed in his stomach. Up he leaped again and dashed out of the house to fling himself by the side of the little river. The water was cool to his face and he drank deep, but the water in his stomach turned to steam, so that he swelled and swelled, and presently there was a loud explosion that shook the very hills, and El Enano burst into a thousand pieces.

Deer Season

Lois Lenski

"Elijah's caught a bear!"

Ken came tearing up on the porch. He had been to the store, and Walter Reed had told him. Walter was telling everybody how Elijah came in, shouting:

"By golly, Walter, I got a bear!"

Abby stood still. It must be the same bear. It had gone off into Elijah's woods that night after it left Grammy's.

It was bear season now, since September first. Several men had set box-traps and Elijah had caught the first one.

"He's got it up there in his barnyard, Walter said," Ken went on. "Let's go up and see it."

Dad and the children got in the car, but Mom said no.

"I can live without seeing a bear," she said. She called out after them, "Don't bring it home with you!"

There was great excitement up at Elijah's place. The big metal box-trap rested on some heavy timbers in the shade of the barn, and the bear, half-grown, was inside, behind the bars. It was a handsome animal with glossy hair, gleaming black, its nose brown at the tip. It sat in a corner of the cage, with one paw through the bars. A crowd of curious people had gathered. The Nelsons and the Stebbinses and the Collinses were there, besides others.

"Hi, Elijah!" called Dad. "You chargin' admission?"

"Don't mind if I do!" said Elijah.

He took off his hat, gave it to his grandson, Ollie, and told him to pass it.

"Let's take up a collection for Elijah!" cried one of the men. They began to drop coins into the hat.

Dad turned to Greg.

"He's serious about it. He's charging admission."

Greg laughed. "It's a good show."

Elijah had to tell his story over and over.

"Where did you set your trap, Elijah?" a man asked.

"Way up by them black spruces. See way up there?" Elijah waved his arm toward the mountain, about a mile away. "That's good b'ar country up there. I could hear 'em hootin' from one valley to the next. I set it at the edge of the woods in the meadow. I put in meat with honey on it for bait. The trap was there for only three days when the b'ar found it. He walked in to eat the honey and the trapdoor banged shut. He was caught!"

Elijah picked up a stick and poked it through the bars.

"Wanta hear him growl?" he asked.

The bear moved away when the stick prodded him. He growled and snapped his jaws.

"At first, you should have seen how wild he was," said Elijah. "He bounded and jumped from one side of the cage to the other, tryin' to get out. Then I had a problem — how to get him home. I figured he weighed near five hundred pounds, he was so fat, and that metal box-trap is heavy, too, weighs about three hundred. Who could I get to help me? I wanted some one with a pickup, but the men I asked were too scared to come. One guy didn't even believe I had a b'ar . . ."

"What did you do then, Elijah?"

"Decided to do it myself," Elijah went on. "I had to git the bobsled and team o' horses to bring him out. The horses shied a little when we got close enough they could smell him, but they calmed down. Then two fellers come by and helped me hist the b'ar, cage and all, onto the bobsled and we got him loaded."

Everybody was listening now.

"On the way back, I had to get purty close to the trap when we went through some brush, and he stuck his paw right through the bars and ripped my sweater right down my back!"

Elijah turned around. Sure enough, his sweater was slit in two from top to bottom.

"Did he hurt you, Elijah?" asked Greg.

"Naw, but I wouldn't want him any closer," said Elijah. "Come on, old feller, you hungry?"

Elijah handed out an apple. The bear backed away and would not take it.

"Better not stick your hand in the cage, Elijah," said Lem Collins. "He might grab an arm offa you."

"I ain't scared," said Elijah.

"What you gonna do with him?" called Collins.

"Keep him," said Elijah. "Make a pet outa him."

"Ain't you scared?" Ken asked.

"I'd just as soon put my hand right on a collar on that bear and lead him out in the open," said Elijah. "I ain't scared a mite."

"He don't look very fierce," said Amos.

"Yesterday when he seen all them men," said Elijah, "he gave right up. Knew he couldn't git out. All the fight went right out of him."

"What you feedin' him?" asked Bill Stebbins.

"Coke right outa the bottle." Elijah laughed.

"Little beer, too?"

"I ain't sayin'," said Elijah.

"Better see the Game Warden," said Amos.

"Already have," said Elijah. "I'm gettin' me a permit to keep him. I got to guarantee protection. If he breaks loose and does damage, like killin' somebody's calf, I'll have to pay the bill. But he won't, I'm sure. *This* b'ar, I'm gonna tame him good."

"You sure?" asked Lem.

Elijah laughed.

"You bet your bottom dollar I'm sure," said Elijah. "Why, he's half tamed already."

He picked up an apple, poked it through the bars and called, "Come on, old feller."

The bear got up like a dog, took the apple out of his hand and ate it.

Amos said, "That's more than I'd do — poke my hand in that cage."

"Me, too," said Lem Collins.

A strange man came up, pushing his way through the crowd.

"Wanta sell the bear?" he asked.

"Can't say as I do," said Elijah.

Elijah was proud of his bear and the attention it was causing in the village. It gave him a new importance.

"I'll give you thirty dollars for him," said the man. "Cold cash." He took out a billfold and began to peel off six five-dollar bills.

"Keep your money," said Elijah. "B'ar's not for sale."

The man turned and strode off. His car was parked out by the road. Elijah looked after him.

"Out-o'-stater, I reckon."

Ollie, his grandson, ran out quickly and came back.

"New York State license plate," he said.

"Yup!" said Elijah. "I thought so."

All the time the men were talking, Abby kept looking at the bear. It crouched in the back of the cage, fearful. It was frightened, even if Elijah thought it wasn't. It was not tame at all, just afraid. Hungry, too — that's why it came for the apple. But all its spirit was gone. A cage was no place for a bear, for a big, strong, husky bear like that. It needed a whole forest to roam over, great trees to climb, far away from people and houses and automobiles and villages. What a shame to pen it up! To show it off like a freak in a sideshow, and to even take money for it. To charge admission to see the poor bear. What an insult!

Abby went closer and looked at the bear. She looked into its small eyes. It stared back at her. Its eyes were red and dull — unseeing. It stared but saw nothing. It was thinking of the woods, its rightful home. Would it ever get back there, away from its enemy, man?

"Let's go home," said Dad.

He, too, had seen enough. Ken and Susan and Bunny climbed in the car with him.

"You go on," said Abby. "I'll come later."

"Where you goin'?" asked Susan.

"For a walk in the woods," said Abby.

They drove off and left her.

It was beautiful in the woods now, for all the trees were ablaze with autumn color. Leaves had begun to fall after the early frost and a carpet of red and gold lay on the ground.

Abby wandered at will, pushing her way through the leaves, and stepping over fallen trees and brush. Once she saw a squirrel with a nut in its mouth, hopping from one tree to another. She could hear birds chirping but not singing. Soon they would be going south to escape the cold winter. Maybe she'd see some deer. She walked quietly, hoping to come upon them unawares.

Elijah's woods backed up on the Peck and Otis farms. There were a few woods roads in this area, but they were not much more than trails. Over at the base of the biggest hill was the spring that supplied water to both the farms. It had never been known to go dry.

Abby walked along, kicking stones and branches out of her path. She wished for Hobo — the dog had so loved a long ramble in the woods. And having a dog to share it with, made a ramble so much more exciting. Hobo could always nose up a rabbit, bark at a squirrel, or jump at a frog. If only he would come back again . . .

Suddenly she heard a motor.

It was a small car, not a truck — she knew the difference in the sound. What was a car doing off here in these woods? No car had any business back up here. She'd have to see. What was it up to?

Was somebody up at the sugarhouse?

Sometimes people broke in, perhaps hoping to find cans of maple syrup, or maybe just for fun or mischief. She came closer now. The sugarhouse was all closed up. Everything looked as usual. No signs of vandalism or disturbance.

It might be at the Otises' sugarhouse. She went on up to the brow of the hill, where she could see it. She came to the big split rock at the top of the ridge. Then the memory of that horrible day flooded her — the dogs chasing the deer, Cal Otis with his gun dashing out to shoot them . . . If anybody shot Hobo, it must have been Cal.

Abby looked around carefully, remembering how Cal had scattered her dad's old sap buckets and put new ones in their place. She knew right where the line was — the line between the two farms. Dad had shown her the stakes long ago. The line had run on the west side of the split rock.

She went to look for the stakes, but they were not there. Was she turned around, mistaking west for east? She looked at the sun. It was in the west. No, her directions were right, but the stakes were no longer there.

She walked all around the big rock, and there on the other side — on the side nearest to Dad's sugarhouse, she found the stakes. They were in a neat row, a long distance apart, each one with a pile of stones around it. She looked carefully. The stones had been piled there recently. They were not green and moss-covered. They had no moss on them at all. She studied the stakes in the line. The line went off at an angle, not straight as before. She followed the stakes. They ran to the northeast — east of the hemlock woods. She saw that some of the trees had been chopped down.

The girl came back in alarm. She had made a discovery. The boundary line that her great-grandfather had squabbled over, had been changed again — and only one person could have done it, Cal Otis. Abby felt like crying.

Was Grammy right? Did people never change?

Then she heard the car's motor again.

What on earth was a car doing up here in the woods? It must be a small one, to get through on the brushy trails. Who was in it and what did they want? Where was it? She walked faster now and before long she saw it — a gravel road, a new one leading up to the hemlock woods. It was the road the Town had voted on Town Meeting Day, to build up over Cedar Mountain. But she had no time to think of that now.

The car — what car? A sudden flash came to her. *Deer-jackers!* A strange car — the man at Elijah's with the New York State license . . . things began to fit together. Walter Reed at the store had told people to watch out for strange cars.

Mildred Rush, down in town, sat by her window every day. It was a grandstand seat for the whole main street. From it she could see every car that entered or left the village. She made a list of all the strange cars. Everybody in town knew the color and make of everybody else's car, of course. A strange car with an out-of-state license plate had to have a reason for coming to town.

This was deer-jacking season, Abby knew. Down at the store, the men talked of nothing else. They told of one woman who was trying to catch deer-jackers. Whenever she saw a strange car, she jumped in her own, barefooted if need be, and followed it, until she was satisfied it was not in some mischief. She kept in close touch with the Game Warden and Sheriff.

121

Abby knew all about deer-jacking. She had heard the talk. At this time of year, people in Deer Valley talked of little else. It was not pleasant talk. Deer found butchered and hidden behind stone walls or in the river, and the culprits getting off scot-free. It was an unpopular subject that Mom had banned completely. Deer-jacking could not be mentioned at home.

Everybody was out of patience with Wes Rogers, the Game Warden. He always had to have proof. He could not do a thing unless the culprit was caught with the goods (venison) on him or in his car. Then and then only would he be fined a hundred dollars and his deer-hunting license taken away from him.

Abby listened again for the car, but all was quiet. She had waited too long. She should have followed it when she first heard the sound of the motor. She wandered on. It was getting darker now. A heavy cloud had come up and taken the warmth of the afternoon sun away.

Abby pulled her sweater tighter and shivered.

She had come down the side of the mountain and was still in the woods, on the slope toward the valley where the river flowed. Trees were still high, beginning to lose their leaves, but the woods was not as dense as before.

Abby knew a little island in the river, in a deeply wooded section. It was one of her favorite spots. She wanted to see it again. After that, she'd go on home. She must not be too late and make Mom worry. Walking along, half-dreaming, she was rudely awakened from her revery by the barking of dogs. Several dogs, close at hand, dogs running and yapping and baying, chasing something . . . Where were they and what were they after?

Again, the picture of the dead deer lying on the white snowbank came to her clearly . . . and the vision of Hobo, who liked to chase a rabbit, maybe, but never a deer . . . dogs running and yelping, coming closer and closer . . .

She was down now near the edge of the river. Across, through the young trees, she could see the little island, her favorite secret spot, waiting for her. Why did the dogs have to come just now, when all she wanted was peace and quiet?

The dogs were still back in the woods somewhere. She could hear but not see them, but what met her ears now was a loud crashing of the brush . . . Some kind of animal was being chased, it was running away to be safe . . . to get away from the cruel, merciless dogs . . .

Something crashed through the bushes and trees beside her and went on. It leaped the stones and the rippling waves of the river in one bound and landed on the island. It was pale twilight now, she could hardly see . . .

Now she saw it! There it stood, the biggest deer she had ever seen in her life. It was pure white, as white as snow, and its horns stood up like great white trees with many branches on its beautiful head. It glowed with a shining light.

Abby gasped. It was a vision — the deer was the most beautiful thing she had ever seen or hoped to see, the most beautiful creature God had ever made.

Was this the white deer that all Vermonters talked about, the deer that was the essence of all beauty and the epitome of all desire?

It stood still, an apparition in white, a dream come true, just for a moment. For only a moment. Could she always hold that vision in her mind and heart and never forget it?

Then she heard the dogs again, and she shook, terrified. She must stop them, she must not let them cross to the island. She must help the white deer get away.

"*Hobo, Hobo!*" she called. "*Come here, come here. Don't chase the deer!*" All dogs became suddenly Hobo, the dog she had loved so much.

Quickly she ran to the spot where the deer had entered the water. She picked up rocks and stones, and when the dogs came, angry and snarling, she threw one after the other, as heavy as she could lift. She stood in the deep, cold water and hurled the rocks, stopping the dogs in their tracks. They growled and turned back, dangerous and menacing. She chased them back up the hill again.

When they were gone, she looked again for the deer. She crossed over to the island and ran up on its sandy bank. She saw deer tracks — she saw where it had stood and she followed the path it had taken. It had splashed into the river on the other side of the island and had run up on a rocky bank. She climbed up . . . but could find no more tracks. It was dark now, too dark to see.

The mystic white deer with the treelike horns was gone. She knew she would never see its like again.

Suddenly, Abby saw that the sun had set and it was already dark. She had a long way to go to get home and Mom would be worried. Dad, too, as he knew she had gone for a walk in the woods.

She crossed a meadow to get to the road. Before she got there, she heard voices, and down in a hollow on the near side of a rock wall, she saw the dim figures of two men. Parked on the other side of the wall was a small black car.

All thought of the white deer vanished.

"*Deer-jackers!*" Abby said to herself. "Golly! What can I do?"

She knew if she ran home to call Dad, she would be too late. They would be up and away long before Dad or Wes Rogers could get back. The Game Warden was never where you wanted him to be at a particular time. You could never get him quickly. There was no house nearer than Grammy's and this was nothing to worry Grammy about.

She would have to do it herself.

"I'll catch them in the act!" Abby said grimly. "I can at least scare the daylights out of them!"

She had no fear. The fact that she was only twelve and the jackers were two grown men, lawbreakers, never entered her head. She felt only the savage anger that every Vermonter feels when the deer herd is being taken illegally.

Abby came as close as she dared. She stood on a little hillock above the hollow and shouted in a loud voice:

"*What are you doing down there?*"

It was enough.

A big bundle went flying through the air into the bushes. Two men leaped the stone wall and jumped into the waiting car. The next minute, the car, without headlights, was speeding across the meadow. It turned at an opening in a hedgerow and entered the road. Now its lights came on, as it headed away from the village, escaping over one of the obscure mountain roads.

Abby ran home as fast as she could go. Breathless and panting, she broke in on the family at the supper table.

Before Mom could say a word about how late she was, Abby gasped out one word: "*Deer-jackers!*"

Dad jumped up out of his chair and shouted, "Where?"

He and Greg followed her as she ran back to the hollow in the meadow. Dad had grabbed his gun and Greg a flashlight, and they soon located the bundle. It was freshly butchered venison wrapped in butcher-shop paper. The refuse from the illegally killed deer had been crudely buried in a hole in the hollow.

Dad and Greg looked at the bundle by flashlight, but did not touch it.

"I'll leave it here," said Dad. "Wes Rogers must pick it up himself."

Again as in many deer-jacking cases, nothing came of it. The Game Warden arrived next day, recovered the bundle of venison from the bushes, and took it away. He dug up the deer carcass, and retrieved the hide and took it to be registered. The State kept a record of all deer killed legally or illegally. The holes in the hide indicated the type of gun used.

Not till the next day did Abby tell the rest of her story.

"I saw a deer with twenty points!" she said quietly.

"You're crazy!" said Greg.

"Don't believe you," said Ken.

"Ten points is the largest around here now," said Dad.

Abby did not dare say the deer was pure white, as white as snow, for fear of being teased about it. Were white deer real or imaginary? Those who saw them were accused of having a vivid imagination, of telling tall tales. To satisfy herself, Abby spoke to the Game Warden when he came.

"Are there really any white deer, Wes?"

"Sure thing — albinos!" said Wes. "Usually spotted brown and white, something like a Texas pony."

"I mean *all white,* as white as snow," Abby said, "with big white antlers like trees? With twenty points?"

Wes grinned. He was a man of few words.

"Hardly!" he said.

"But *white?*" asked Abby.

"Yup!" he said. "You're right."

Abby knew it was real, she had not dreamed it. She did not tell how she had seen it on her secret island, but she took Dad up to the sugarhouse and showed him the stakes that had been moved. He followed the new stakes all the way to the hemlock woods. He saw the new road over Cedar Mountain and the trees in the woods that had been chopped down.

The stakes *had* been moved, Dad agreed. But he scratched his head uncertainly.

"Are you gonna do something?" Abby asked.

"Dunno," said Dad.

"You know who did it, don't you?" asked Abby.

"Yup," said Dad. "Only one man could be so mean — Cal Otis."

"Well, then . . ."

"I'll see," said Dad.

"He shot Hobo, too," Abby said. "Don't forget that."

Dad just stared at her.

"You're a Peck and he's an Otis!" said Abby angrily.

"That's just the trouble," said Dad. "That's why I've got to move careful, so I don't miss my step."

"Oh!" said Abby.

◆ ◆ ◆

"Mom, make Greg let me try it," said Susan.

"Try what?" asked Mom.

"Try shootin' with his gun."

"Oh, dear, no!" said Mom. "Do I have to live through deer season again?"

"Guess you will, Mom," said Greg, with a grin. "Don't know how you'll avoid it."

Bear season was on now, and would soon be followed by deer season. All the men and boys were getting ready for it. Greg practiced every day after school with his .22 gauge rifle.

He set tin cans on a log and shot them off. He tried throwing them up in the air and hitting them. He would see a fly on the garage door and shoot at it. He made a bulls-eye out of cardboard, with a red circle in the middle and practiced hitting it. He shot across the meadow against the hill, when no one was in sight.

Susan begged to try it.

"You don't know which end of the gun to shoot," said Greg.

"I do, too. I can point it," said Susan. "And I know what I am shooting at."

"You don't know where to put the shells in!" said Greg.

Susan teased so much, Greg sat down on the porch to show her.

"Now in a shotgun," he said, "the shots all spread out. That's what we use for birds or chicken hawks. But a .22 rifle will shoot a mile."

Ken crowded close and listened, too. He had heard it all before, and was not too bad a shot himself. Bunny said, "Show me, too." Abby got up and walked away.

"Don't you want to practice, Abby?" asked Greg.

"No," said Abby. "No shooting for me."

"What's got into you?" asked Greg. "You said you were going to get a deer license this year."

"Costs too much," said Abby. "I haven't got three fifty."

"You said you were going to shoot a deer this year," added Ken.

"Changed my mind," said Abby.

She walked off toward the barn.

Flash stayed in the barn all the time now. Abby had been neglecting the fawn lately. She must go out and play with her. She ran on, her sneakers hitting the ground lightly. She was sick of guns and shooting. She felt like Mom — how could she bear to live through another deer season? How could she listen to all the lurid tales of deer being shot and how much they weighed and who got the biggest and where they found it . . .

Then suddenly, halfway to the barn, she heard a shot, the sharp hard crack of a rifle.

As if it had hit her own body, she stopped that instant. She turned and tore back to the house. Susan . . . oh, what had happened to Susan? Why hadn't she stopped it — those crazy boys, trying to teach little Susan, only nine, how to shoot! And Bunny looking on, little three-year-old Bunny!

There on the porch they were all standing like puppets, faces white as sheets! Dad was there, too — where had he come from? He held the gun in his hand and he was shouting at Greg.

Abby stared. Susan was crying, but she did not seem to be hurt. Bunny was in Mom's arms, inside the kitchen door. They were both crying. Ken's face looked drawn and scared. Greg stuttered, trying to explain.

129

No one was shot. No one was hurt, thank goodness!

Ken pointed. There was a big hole in the floor, where the bullet went through — two inches away from his own small foot.

"I was holding it down . . . ," Greg said, "the way you always said to do . . ."

"Thank God," said Dad, "you remembered *one* thing at least."

Greg went on, "I was just holding it, and Ken reached out to take it and bumped it . . ."

"What did you FORGET?" demanded Dad.

"That it was loaded."

Ken spoke in a low voice.

Dad was disgusted.

"After all the trouble I've taken with you boys!"

Mom spoke from inside.

"They're too young to be foolin' with guns."

It was the old argument over and over again.

Abby ran back to the barn, so she would not have to listen. It was an argument that never got answered. All Vermont boys went deer hunting. Practically all of them got guns at the age of twelve — .22 rifles that could shoot a mile. The only instruction they got was random words of advice from their own fathers.

Abby ran out to the barn and called Flash by name. The tame fawn came running to meet her. Abby put her arms around the fawn's neck and let her nibble her ear.

After Flash had grown too large to stay in the garage, and after she had eaten off a bucket of Mom's petunias, she had to be kept permanently in the barn. There she ran loose with the cows and horses. She stayed there, even with the barn doors open. At first, she never seemed to want to run away. She would come out, look around, then when Abby fixed her a panful of grain, she would come back in again to eat.

Only once did she run away. She ran out into the corn field and stayed all night. The children hunted for her till well past bedtime, but could not find her. Abby went to bed sorrowful. But the next morning, there was Flash back in the barn again. The barn was her home.

Flash was feeling frisky today. Abby played hide-and-seek with her. She ran and hid behind the grain bags and Flash came and found her. It was fun trying to hide from the fawn, then jumping out and crying *Boo!* The fawn capered happily about, enjoying it, too.

On Sunday, Dad took the family to the Chicken Shoot.

It was held at Buckbee's farm over on the Johnson Road. Jim Buckbee bought chickens wholesale and sold chances at twenty-five cents each to attract the hunters.

Mom did not want to go, but Dad said, "Greg needs all the practice he can get. If that boy's going to handle a gun, he has to learn how."

A large crowd had gathered. The men came to shoot, and the women and children to visit. The Buckbee children had built a stand, where they sold pop and hot dogs. A large bull's-eye target had been set up in an empty field against a high hill, and distances were paced off. Guns kept popping all afternoon, as the men and boys took turns. Abby and Susan met girls they knew and went into the Buckbee house with them.

Mom was getting ready to go home. Bunny was cross from missing her nap, and Ken said he had the earache. Mom started toward the car, when Myrtie Otis suddenly appeared. Mom had not seen her before.

The women talked together in a low voice.

"Oh, I don't know how I possibly could. . . ," Mom said.

Abby had come out of the house, ready to go home. Myrtie Otis was making trouble again. What was she pestering Mom about? Abby went up close. Myrtie Otis had turned away. She was crying now. Her eyes were red and she was sniffling. She walked right past Abby without speaking.

Abby heard Mom say, "I'll think about it."

About what? Mom did not say.

Greg came up all excited. He had hit the bull's-eye and won a chicken. He held it up proudly.

Dad was proud, too. Greg had redeemed himself after that near-accident.

"Let's go home," said Abby. Susan came and joined her.

They all drove home.

On the morning after Halloween, Abby and Susan started out early. They wanted to stop at the store before the school bus came. Susan needed pencils and an eraser, and Abby wanted a hair band and a nail file. On their walk to the store, they saw gates taken off, a bicycle on a porch roof, and a car overturned.

They giggled at all the Halloween mischief the boys had done the night before. Greg had been out late with them, they knew that. He was not up yet when they left home.

"Did the boys do anything bad to you, Walter?" Abby asked.

"Nope," said the storekeeper. "I locked everything up tight. I'm onto all their tricks."

The girls made their purchases and went out on the porch of the store to wait for the school bus.

Suddenly a car came speeding down the road and stopped with a screech of the brakes. It was an old broken-down Ford, covered with mud. Anybody could recognize it on sight. It belonged to Elijah Woodburn.

There was no doubt about it. The girls stared in astonishment.

Elijah was in the front seat shouting:

"Somebody shot my b'ar! By George, somebody shot my b'ar!"

His shouts brought Walter Reed out from the store.

Elijah leaped from his car, dressed all in white! The girls giggled. There he was, wearing his long white woolen underwear! He was not even dressed! The October nights were beginning to get chilly, and he must have felt the cold badly to have put on his long Johns so early. He paid no attention to the girls.

Elijah was thundering mad. He shook his fists as he shouted, telling Walter his story. He had been wakened by hearing shots at his barn. When he ran out he found the cage door open and the bear gone.

"Them young squirts come and let my tame b'ar outa the cage and shot him. I heard half-a-dozen shots!" he cried.

"Did you find the body?" demanded Walter.

"Nope," said Elijah, "but I heard all the shots."

"You ain't got no proof they shot him," said Walter.

"I looked everywhere, but I couldn't find hide nor hair of that beast," said Elijah. "I been huntin' for him ever since daybreak."

"Reckon them boys couldn't aim very good," said Walter. "Your b'ar just took off for the woods, after they unlocked the gate and opened it up. He probably chased the boys and gave them a good scare."

"You sound as if you know all about it!" said Elijah.

Walter began to protest.

"Don't stand there yakkin'," cried Elijah. "Call the State Police. I want them young squirts put in jail!" Elijah had no telephone at home, so had to depend on the one at the store.

Walter went inside. People began to come up and laughed at Elijah's attire, and still more at the tale he had to tell. He was still sputtering: "I had a cash offer of thirty dollars for that b'ar, and now he's gone . . ."

The school bus came along and Abby and Susan got on. They had exciting news to tell. All day long, the children at school could think and talk of nothing else but Elijah's bear.

The bear was not shot, after all. If it had been Elijah would certainly have been able to find its body. Abby was glad. She remembered the sad, dull look in its unseeing eyes. How happy it must be to be free again — to roam the woods at will and climb the big trees in the forest.

Abby was glad the boys had let it loose.

But Elijah was not.

The bear, his pride and joy, was gone.

Dad went up to see him, to offer to help. Elijah was unhappy and depressed.

"Yup! State Police came," he said. "Told me I'd got to have two witnesses, said I'd got to prove it. But I didn't see them young squirts break the padlock, nor shoot them bullets to scare the b'ar and make him run out. How could I see it, when I was in bed sound asleep and snoring? But I know who done it . . ."

"How do you know?" asked Amos.

"Ollie, my grandson, told me," said Elijah. "They come up just 'fore dark yesterday, to look things over. Ollie seen 'em and talked to 'em. They looked at the cage and at the padlock. They saw just how it was fixed. If Ollie'd a told me . . ."

"You'll have to trap another bear," said Amos.

"I know who done it," Elijah repeated. He looked at Amos hard. "I don't like to name names, but I tell you, Amos Peck, 'birds of a feather flock together'. . ."

"What do you mean?" asked Amos.

"You'd better watch out what kind o' company your boy's keepin'," said Elijah.

Amos looked up in surprise. "You mean Greg?"

"Yup! I mean that young squirt o' yours, Greg Peck," said Elijah. "Them older boys might git him in trouble. Better keep your eye on him."

"Are you sure Greg was with them?" asked Amos. "Can you prove it?"

"Nope, not in court, I can't," said Elijah. "Wisht I could."

"Was one of them Rupe Otis?"

Elijah shook his head. "I'm not tellin'."

That night Dad had a talk with Greg. Greg admitted he had gone up with Rupe Otis, Bert Reed, and Jed Collins before dark. They had seen the bear and looked over the trap to see how it was locked and had talked to Ollie. He had done some mischief with Jed Collins, but had come home early and was in bed asleep before midnight.

Mom said she had looked at the clock when he came in and it was eleven P.M. That proved it — Greg was innocent.

Everybody was relieved, especially Dad.

Abby told Greg, "I'm glad the bear got loose."

"So'm I," said Greg. "If I meet him walkin' down the highway, I'll take a potshot at him."

"You'd kill him?" cried Abby. "Just when he got loose and is enjoying life again?"

"I told you I want a bearskin rug to put by my bed," said Greg. "Something nice and warm to step out on, on the cold winter mornings."

"Your aim's not good enough," teased Abby.

"Yes, it is!" bragged Greg. "I hit the bull's-eye. I won a chicken!"

Two days later, Mom gave the family a surprise.

"I've got a job," she said.

"You? A job? Where? What for?" The questions came thick and fast. "Away from home? Every day, all week long?"

Mom had a hard time explaining.

"I'm needed," she said.

"You're needed *here*," said Dad, as surprised as the children.

"But this is a special case," said Mom. "It's an old lady, and she's quite childish and the family can't find anyone to take the responsibility. One person has to give her whole time to it — daytime. There's another nurse for the night." She paused. "I think I'll like it for a change."

"But what about *us*?" asked Abby. "Who'll look after *us*? You won't go off and leave Bunny here alone, I hope."

Dad was always busy on the farm or at the sawmill and now he'd be spending all his time in the woods, with the hunting season coming on.

"I can have Bunny with me," said Mom. "She'll be no trouble. They promised me that."

Everybody looked unhappy. Home without Mom would not be home at all.

"They're well off," Mom said. "They'll pay me well."

"It's not that," Dad began. "I'm not rich, but still I make enough to pay our bills. I don't need to let my wife go out to work."

"It's for only a short time," said Mom. "I'll get a good rest out of it."

The boys began to grumble.

"Who'll make Ken mind?" asked Greg.

"Who'll call Greg down?" asked Ken.

"Dad will be here, at least for meals," said Mom, "and in the evenings. I'll come home evenings, too."

"Who'll COOK?" cried Abby.

"YOU will!" teased Greg.

"Yes, *you*," said Mom. "It's time you began to take some responsibility, Abby."

"Don't go, Mom," begged Susan, crying.

But all their coaxing was of no avail. Mom took her job.

As everybody began to get ready for the hunting season, the whole village came to life. Excitement and drama came into the lives of every family. Men and boys sat on porches with cleaning rods and cloths, oiling up their rifles and sighting them in. Red caps and red jackets came out of trunks, ready to be put on. Everybody was busy buying ammunition, gloves, and boots. Walter Reed did a thriving business. The hunters walked and drove around looking for deer signs, places where bucks had rubbed their horns on little saplings, and for deer tracks. They listened intently to every radio weather forecast, hoping for a little snow.

The day before the season opened, the deer were plentiful in all the meadows in Deer Valley, creatures of beauty and grace to be admired and loved by all. But after the first shot on the first day of deer season, all the deer promptly vanished from sight. As if guided by some hidden instinct, they disappeared as completely as if they had never existed.

On the first night of deer-hunting season, a Hunters' Supper was held. A sign in the store told about it:

Come as you are
HUNTERS' SUPPER
Benefit of Boy Scouts
Hot Dishes
Home-Baked Goods

It was held in the Community Hall and everybody came. Not only all the families of the village and the surrounding area, but relatives, city folk, and out-of-staters who had come to camp nearby and hunt. The women brought food and everybody ate all they could hold. Two hundred dollars was made for the Boy Scouts. Dad and Greg went, but Mom and Abby and the children stayed home.

A little in advance of the deer season, the Deer Hunters' Reunion had been held, a get-together for the purpose of making up a Deer Pool All the men who loved to hunt met at the

Town Hall. Each man put in one dollar, the total sum to be used for prizes at the end of the season. Walter Reed prepared a large card on which to enter the men's names. Coffee and doughnuts were served, and the men slapped their knees and laughed, telling deer stories.

At the end of deer season, the man who got the heaviest buck would receive two-thirds of the money in the pool. And the man with the smallest would get the other third. Walter was to keep the card at the store and enter on it the weights of the deer killed, and the number of points of its horns. Walter had a large scale in the back of his store for weighing the deer.

The hunters stayed all evening and told deer stories, each one topping the one before. Dad and Greg came home all excited, repeating tales they had heard.

"Oh, if I can only live through the next sixteen days," cried Mom, "I'll be happy! Sixteen days — it can't come to an end too soon for me."

The Hunters' Supper was only the beginning.

On the designated day, the first shot was fired at six o'clock. Then the whole world suddenly went mad. Overnight the once quiet and peaceful Deer Valley became crowded with cars and people. Carloads of gun-happy hunters converged on all the country roads. In no time at all, they passed through the village with carcasses of deer draped over their hoods. The officers of the law, Game Wardens, Sheriffs, and State Police worked overtime, often not getting to bed at all, but snatching a few hours of sleep in their cars. It was an exciting, but hectic and dangerous, time for everybody.

Men and boys got up each day at dawn and drove off by car or truck. Some were "road hunters," riding the roads, looking.

Sometimes they stopped, jumped out and shot at something moving in the brush. Each hunter had his favorite location, his secret spot, picked out during months of summer exploring, where he knew the greatest number of deer congregated. They all knew that the actual range of any deer is over a very restricted area — not usually more than one square mile.

Dad and Greg were as eager as any of the hunters and had everything ready. Greg knew just what they would need — a rope, or barring that, a belt out of a pair of their pants, a hunting knife, dry matches to use if lost, in case they might have to stay overnight, and a shoestring out of one of their shoes to tie the deer-tag on . . . if they got a deer. And, of course, they had to wear red caps and jackets.

Dad made Ken stay at home and Ken said he didn't want to go anyway. He came indoors in his spare time and read comic books.

Each day was a big adventure. Dad and Greg roamed the woods, exploring all those special places where the deer were supposed to be. Once, in passing Elijah Woodburn's place, they saw one of his cows out in the barnyard. On the cow's back was a large placard, with the word COW printed in black letters two feet high.

Dad and Greg roared and teased Elijah about it.

"That's for them city slickers!" said Elijah. "They don't know a deer when they see one!"

Each day Dad and Greg returned home empty-handed and told how the deer had eluded them. They had all kinds of complaints, the chief one being the lack of snow, making it impossible to track the deer. Nobody could get near one by walking. The frozen leaves crackled loudly and gave the deer warning.

The report was dismal — no snow, freezing cold, and deer scarcer than hens' teeth!

But that did not stop them from going to the store each evening. They had to see who got a deer, learn where he got it and how much it weighed. All the hunters gathered there to sympathize with each other. Almost every deer taken was just unlucky enough to be in a meadow when someone drove by. Or when a hunter was standing still on a runway.

Abby was glad now that Mom had her job. A man they did not know came and took her and Bunny to town every morning in his car, away from the intense hunting atmosphere. Mom had to keep her mind on her patient, the old lady who needed constant attention. Mom had no time to think of deer hunting all day long.

Mom's absence put real responsibility on Abby. As soon as she came home from school, she and Susan ran straight to the house. There they found a list Mom had made out for them: "Wash dishes. Sweep kitchen floor. Peel potatoes. Dust bedrooms. Make beds, etc." No more running off into the woods for a ramble.

The woods was a dangerous place now, dangerous for animal and man alike. Children were kept indoors, no one went for walks.

Mom said, "In deer season, we keep the dogs in, we keep the children in, and we keep the cows in."

The first snow came and cold bleak winds, bringing the last of the leaves off all the trees. There was little sun and on most days, the sky was heavy with clouds. Nature was in a cheerless mood, giving a foretaste of the long hard winter ahead. The only bright note was the red of the hunters' caps and jackets.

Each day Abby was concerned for Flash. Each day, after school, she ran to the barn to feed her, to be sure that the doors and windows were locked and the pet fawn was safe inside.

When Dad and Greg complained about not getting a deer, Mom and Abby looked at each other and smiled.

Mom looked around the room at the mounted deer heads on the wall. There was the fourteen-point buck killed by Grandpa Seth many years ago, Amos's twelve-pointer and his brother Ellis's ten-pointer. Also various mounted horns without heads.

"No more deer heads allowed in my house!" cried Mom.

Dad looked at her out of the corner of his eye and chuckled.

◆ ◆ ◆

"Thanksgiving?" asked Abby. "What's there to be thankful for?"

"Dad's fattening a turkey," said Susan.

"The deer season's gonna last forever," said Abby bitterly. "Thanksgiving will never come."

"Oh, yes, it will," said Susan. "It always comes at the end of deer season. Just you wait and see! Mom says she's going to have a big party."

"Gracious!" said Abby. "I hope not. I don't want a house full of company. I just want peace and quiet. I don't ever want to hear the sound of a gun again."

Susan went and told Grammy. Grammy was busy, mixing a cake.

"A big party for Thanksgiving?" cried Grammy. "That's fine. I'll be there with bells on. Who's coming?"

"Well, I don't like to mention their names," said Susan. "You might not want to come if I told you."

"All the Pecks and the Pattersons?" asked Grammy.

"No," said Susan, "not the kinfolk, Mom said. Just neighbors."

"Neighbors for Thanksgiving?" cried Grammy. "Thanksgiving's the time for kinfolk."

"I know, but Mom said . . ."

"Which neighbors?" demanded Grammy.

"You'll get mad if I tell you," said Susan.

"Oh — I know! The Otises!" cried Grammy. "She's inviting the Otis tribe, I bet! Just like your mom."

"Yes, but she wants YOU, too!" said Susan.

Grammy laughed.

"Oh, I wouldn't miss the fun for anything!" she said. "Gettin' the Pecks and the Otises together is just like settin' matches to fireworks! The sparks sure will fly!" Grammy chuckled with glee.

Mom's job ended as suddenly as it began.

"The old lady died," she said. "And the whole family were so grateful to me, just because I helped them out. They couldn't thank me enough."

The children and Dad were glad to get Mom back again. But they did not see much more of her than when she had been working. She was always going off somewhere. She came home sometimes with Dad in his car late in the afternoon, and had to hurry to get supper. She and Dad were up to something. No one could guess what was going on. Even Abby could not guess.

Abby asked Greg, and Greg was no help. He had no idea, either.

143

Several times Abby saw a strange young man in Dad's car. They drove away quickly and never came to the house at all. When she asked Dad where he had been, he said, "Up in the woods."

But he had not taken his gun, and he had done no hunting. He refused to let Greg go hunting, too, though Greg's pals, Bert Reed and Jud Collins, came and asked if he could go. Dad told them, "Greg needs more gun practice. Next year maybe."

The boys went away disappointed.

Something unusual was going on, but Abby decided not to worry. Mom and Dad had something on their minds, and she knew they would take care of it, and tell when they were ready.

Her own worry was a very personal one.

What could she do with Flash?

All through the hunting season, she guarded the fawn faithfully. Flash stayed safe and secure in the barn. But she was growing fast now and could not be kept there forever. She was a wildling and should have her freedom. Could she take care of herself in the woods? Could she find her own food, she who had been fed from bottle and hand? Could she defend herself from her enemies, she who had known only human kindness and love?

Abby thought things over.

If she let Flash go in late fall, how could she find food through the winter, when it was so scarce? How could she manage the snowdrifts? How would she get along with the other deer? Abby had heard tales that a deer conditioned to man was never accepted by the deer herd. Flash would be an outcast . . . the thought was unbearable.

One day Dad said, "You'll soon have to let Flash go."

"I know," said Abby. "After deer season is over. Will she be able to take care of herself?"

Dad shook his head. "Hard to say."

"Then I won't . . ."

"She'll have to find a mate and rear a family," said Dad.

"But how . . ."

Dad put his hand on Abby's shoulder.

"Let's call the Game Warden in and ask him about it."

It was good to put the final decision in someone else's hands.

Wes Rogers came and they talked it over. Wes understood the problem. He was blunt and he spoke the truth.

"The herd will never accept her," he said. "She won't be able to find food in the wintertime. She'll die in a month or two — unless dogs catch her or someone shoots her."

Abby's eyes filled with tears.

"That's why the Game Wardens don't encourage people to take baby fawns and raise them," he said. "It always ends in grief."

"Oh, Wes, can't we do something?" cried Abby.

"We usually tell the family to turn the pet fawn loose in the woods. . . ," Wes began.

"Isn't there someplace we could take her where she'd be safe?" asked Abby.

"Well. . . ," said Wes, slowly. "The State Fish and Game Department might take a pet fawn to the Bennington Soldiers Home. That's about the only enclosed place in Vermont that's allowed to keep wild deer. There's another place at Fairlee, but it's full up. You might ask at Bennington. They might take Flash."

"Oh, Wes, thank you!" cried Abby.

So Amos made a trip to Bennington.

Instead of being a sad day when Flash left, it was a happy one. The children put a wreath of chrysanthemums around her neck, played hide-and-seek with her, and fondled her for the last time. Then she was loaded into the truck and taken away.

It was sad for Abby to watch her go. But she smiled bravely — it was better than to see her disappear in the hard, cold, unfriendly winter woods. Flash would be loved and cared for, she would be with people. Flash would be safe from harm.

Abby was disturbed about Mom's plans for Thanksgiving. Why had she invited the Otises, of all people? There were still all those quarrels unresolved — all those deliberate meannesses that only the Otises were capable of. Must one overlook them all and pretend they did not exist?

She went straight to Mom and asked her about it.

"Cal is after Dad's timber, Mom!" said Abby. "He's changed all the boundary stakes, he's had the town build that road over Cedar Mountain just so he can haul out Dad's timber. He's started chopping the trees down already. *I saw them!* I followed the new stakes and they go right down on the *east* side of the woods and not on the west."

Mom sat down to answer.

"Grandfather Seth Peck fought with Mark Otis over that timber long ago," she said. "Grammy can tell you all about it. Grandpa got up on the stone wall and threatened Mark Otis with his shotgun! Mark had logs cut, and five teams of horses up there ready to haul them out. But he didn't. Seth stopped him — with a shotgun!"

Abby grinned.

"He stopped him! He kept his timber!"

"Now Dad and Cal are fighting over the same timber," said Mom. "Do you want your dad to get up on a stone wall and shoot at Cal Otis to make him stop?"

"No, I don't," said Abby.

"I don't either," said Mom. "There are other ways of settling disputes."

"But he's got to be stopped," said Abby. *"He can't take Dad's timber — I'll stop him myself!"*

Mom looked at her.

"Did you ever happen to think that maybe it's *Cal's* timber?" asked Mom quietly. "That maybe the Pecks are in the wrong?"

"Cal's timber?" cried Abby in astonishment. "I always thought it was Dad's . . ."

"So did I," said Mom, "but now we're going to make certain. We're going to end this quarreling for good. I don't want to see Greg and Ken spending their lives fighting Rupe and Herb Otis. Nor you and Susan forever quarreling with Cassie Otis. We're neighbors and we've got to learn to be *friends.*"

"*Friends!*" Abby sniffed.

Mom smiled. "Don't worry, girl. Dad and I are settling this feud for good and all."

Abby felt better, although she had no idea what Mom meant. Nor did she find out until Thanksgiving Day. She worked hard and helped Mom and Aunt Martha, Uncle Ellis's wife, with all the preparations — the cleaning, the baking, and then getting the big table set up and ready. That morning the house was filled with delicious smells and everybody was happy and in good spirits.

Grammy came over and sat in the front room, visiting with Myrtie Otis as if they had been lifelong friends. Myrtie had no complaints to mention — she had forgotten her old ones and could not think up any new ones. Even Cassie and Herb were on their best behavior. Herb could not think up a single mean trick to play.

What had caused this sudden change of heart in these dyed-in-the-wool enemies? Abby could not understand it. After all the weeks and months of strain and suspicion, the winds of hate seemed to have blown away. Like the calm after a storm, trouble faded and peace had descended on the two contentious families.

What caused it? Abby wanted to know. But everybody was too busy to answer any questions.

During the morning, while the women were busy in the kitchen, the Peck and Otis men and boys disappeared. They came back at noontime, weary and hungry after a long hard walk. The strange young man, whom Abby had seen in Dad's car, came with them. He sat at the end of the table beside Dad. After the first part of the dinner was over, he spoke.

He said he was a lawyer, and that he had searched the old town records and read the original deeds. He and a surveyor had re-established the boundary to a new location, to conform to the records. Amos and Cal had tramped the boundaries and been convinced that he was right.

"Where does the line go?" demanded Abby. "To the west or the east of the hemlock woods?"

The young man laughed.

"Neither," he said. "It goes right through the middle. The woods lot doesn't belong to Peck nor to Otis. Each owns half!"

Everybody laughed.

"For three generations the Otises have been trying to get it away from the Pecks," said Dad.

"And the Pecks have been fighting the Otises," added Cal.

"They just kept on feuding!" added Dad, with a hearty laugh.

Grammy had been listening intently, trying to follow the conversation.

"Who d'you say that woods lot belongs to, young feller?" she asked, turning to the lawyer.

"Half to Peck and half to Otis," said the man. "We've struck a new line — iron stakes this time — right down through the middle."

"Good gracious!" cried Grammy. "Old Abner Peck would turn over in his grave if he heard that. He thought he owned it and wanted to hand it down to his children and grandchildren and great-grandchildren. Could old Abner Peck have made a mistake?"

"It looks that way," said the lawyer.

Grammy turned to Cal Otis.

"Why, Cal," she said, "so you're gettin' half of old Abner's timber. Do you think you really deserve it?"

Cal had a hard time to think of an answer.

"I always wanted that woods lot," he said. "I'm glad to get half of it. It was Serena who made me stop fightin' and cussin' and listen to reason. And she did more than that. She left her own family and come over and took care o' my pore old mother when her mind was wandering and no one else could do a thing with her . . ."

Abby sat up. So Mom had been nursing Grandma Otis! She had never told them who it was.

"I was downright grateful to her for that," said Cal.

"You'd ought to be," said Grammy.

Mom was embarrassed.

"I was glad to do it," she said. "I loved Grandma Otis. She used to give me doughnuts when I was a little girl and I never forgot it. But I had a reason, too, for going to work."

Everybody listened.

"I wanted to earn the money," Mom said, "to pay for a surveyor and a lawyer. I made up my mind the old boundary dispute should be settled, but not by a shotgun and hatred and revenge, but by law and order. That's what I wanted the money for."

Everybody was quiet around the table, even the children.

"The Pecks and Otises have been neighbors for three generations, going on the fourth," said Mom. "It's time now for them to be *friends*."

Everybody clapped.

"My goodness!" cried Grammy. "Do you mean to say the Pecks and the Otises are gonna kiss and make up? They're not gonna fight any more? Why, that'll take all the spice outa life! Do you really mean to say that the Peck-Otis feud is OVER?"

"Yes, it's over!" said Dad. "For good and all."

"Yup, it's over," said Cal Otis.

The men got up and shook hands.

Myrtie slipped out of her chair. Mom had gotten up to bring on the mince and pumpkin pies. She set them on the table.

Myrtie put her arms around Mom and cried.

Only Grammy had her reservations. She turned to Abby and whispered: "A leopard never changes his spots!"

After the Otises went back home again, the house seemed very quiet. Off on the mountains, guns were still popping, for Thanksgiving Day was the last day of the deer season.

The sound made Abby think of Hobo, her dog. She had given up thinking he might still be alive. She knew now he was gone.

She went to Dad.

"I'm glad the boundary fight is settled, Dad," she said. "I can forgive Cal Otis for all the trouble he made, now that the whole thing is settled by law. But there's one thing I can't ever forgive . . . He shot Hobo and I still hate him for that."

Dad put his two hands on the girl's shoulders.

"You'll have to forgive that, too," he said. "Remember Mom's rule: forgive and forget."

"But he had no right to . . ."

"Hon," said Dad, "remember what I told you that first day when Elijah brought Hobo' s collar back?"

"What did you tell me?"

"That Elijah didn't shoot him and . . ."

"What else?"

"That Cal didn't either," Dad added.

"You are only guessing," said Abby.

"I *know!*" said Dad. "I can prove it."

"How?"

"I know who shot Hobo," said Dad.

Abby would not look up. Did she sense what he was going to say?

"Who?" she asked in a low voice. She had to know.

"*I* did," said Dad.

At last she knew. Sometimes she had suspected it, but she had not been sure. It had been easier to have a scapegoat, to blame it on Cal, to blame Cal for everything.

"I had to," said Dad.

"I know," said Abby.

She leaned on Dad's shoulder, crying softly. Dad put his arms around her, to comfort her.

Hobo was gone, but she would never forget him.

The Magic Ball

Charles J. Finger

A cold-eyed witch lived in the Cordilleras and when the first snow commenced to fall she was always full of glee, standing on a rock, screaming like a wind-gale and rubbing her hands. For it pleased her to see the winter moon, the green country blotted out, the valleys white, the trees snow-laden, and the waters ice-bound and black. Winter was her hunting time and her eating time, and in the summer she slept. So she was full of a kind of savage joy when there were leaden clouds and drifting gales, and she waited and watched, waited and watched, ever ready to spring upon frost-stiffened creatures that went wandering down to the warmer lowlands.

This witch was a wrinkled creature, hard of eye, thin-lipped, with hands that looked like roots of trees, and so tough was her skin that knife could not cut nor arrow pierce it. In the country that swept down to the sea she was greatly feared, and hated, too. The hate came because by some strange magic she was able to draw children to her one by one, and how she did it no man knew. But the truth is that she had a magic ball, a ball bright and shining and of many colours, and this she left in places where children played, but never where man or woman could see it.

One day, near the lake called Oretta, a brother and sister were at play and saw the magic ball at the foot of a little hill. Pleased with its brightness and beauty Natalia ran to it, intending to pick it up and take it home, but, to her surprise, as she drew near to it the ball rolled away; then, a little way off, came to rest again. Again she ran to it and almost had her hand on it when it escaped, exactly as a piece of thistle-down does, just as she was about to grasp it. So she followed it, always seeming to be on the point of catching it but never doing so, and as she ran her brother Luis followed, careful lest she should come to harm. The strange part of it was that every time the ball stopped it rested close to some berry bush or by the edge of a crystal-clear spring, so that she, like all who were thus led away, always found at the moment of resting something to eat or to drink or to refresh herself. Nor, strangely enough, did she tire, but because of the magic went skipping and running and jumping just as long as she followed the ball. Nor did any one under the spell of that magic note the passing of time, for days were like hours and a night like the shadow of a swiftly flying cloud.

At last, chasing the ball, Natalia and Luis came to a place in the valley where the Río Chico runs between great hills, and it was dark and gloomy and swept by heavy gray clouds. The land was strewn with mighty broken rocks and here and there were patches of snow, and soon great snow flakes appeared in the air. Then boy and girl were terror-struck, for they knew with all the wandering and twisting and turning they had lost their way. But the ball still rolled on, though slower now, and the children followed. But the air grew keener and colder and the sun weaker, so that they were very glad indeed when they came to a black rock where, at last, the ball stopped.

Natalia picked it up, and for a moment gazed at its beauty, but for a moment only. For no sooner had she gazed at it and opened her lips to speak than it vanished as a soap bubble does, at which her grief was great. Luis tried to cheer her and finding that her hands were icy cold led her to the north side of the rock where it was warmer, and there he found a niche like a lap between two great arms, and in the moss-grown cranny Natalia coiled herself up and was asleep in a minute. As for Luis, knowing that as soon as his sister had rested they must set out about finding a way home, he sat down intending to watch. But not very long did he keep his eyes open, for he was weary and sad at heart. He tried hard to keep awake, even holding his eyelids open with his fingers, and he stared hard at a sunlit hilltop across the valley, but even that seemed to make him sleepy. Then, too, there were slowly nodding pine trees and the whispering of leaves, coming in a faint murmur from the mountainside. So, soon, Luis slept.

Natalia, being out of the blustering wind, was very comfortable in the little niche between the great stone arms, and she dreamed that she was at home. Her mother, she thought, was combing her hair and singing as she did so. So she forgot her hunger and weariness, and in her dreamland knew nothing of the bare black rocks and snow-patched hills. Instead, she seemed to be at home where the warm firelight danced on the walls and lighted her father's brown face to a lively red as he mended his horse gear. She saw her brother, too, with his jet-black hair and cherry-red lips. But her mother, she thought, grew rough and careless and pulled her hair, so that she gave a little cry of pain and awoke. Then in a flash she knew where she was and was chilled to the bone with the piercing wind that swept down from the mountain top. Worse still, in front of her stood the old witch of the hills, pointing, pointing, pointing with knotty forefinger, and there were nails on her hands and feet that looked like claws.

Natalia tried to rise, but could not, and her heart was like stone when she found what had happened. It was this: while she slept, the witch had stroked and combed her hair, and meanwhile wrought magic, so that the girl's hair was grown into the rock so very close that she could not as much as turn her head. All that she could do was to stretch forth her arms, and when she saw Luis a little way off she called to him most piteously. But good Luis made no move. Instead, he stood with arms wide apart like one who feels a wall in the dark, moving his hands this way and that. Then Natalia wept, not understanding and little knowing that the witch had bound Luis with a spell, so that there seemed to be an invisible wall around the rock through which he could not pass, try as he would. But he heard the witch singing in her high and cracked voice, and this is what she sang:

"Valley all pebble-sown,
Valley where wild winds moan!
Come, mortals, come.

"Valley so cool and white,
Valley of winter night,
Come, children, come.

"Straight like a shaft to mark,
Come they to cold and dark,
Children of men!"

Then she ceased and stood with her root-like finger upraised, and from nearby came the voice of a great white owl, which took up the song, saying:

"Things of the dark and things without name,
Save us from light and the torch's red flame."

Now all this was by starlight, but the moment the owl had ceased, from over the hill came a glint of light as the pale moon rose, and with a sound like a thunderclap the witch melted into the great rock and the owl flapped away heavily.

"Brother," whispered the girl, "you heard what the owl said?"

"Yes, sister, I heard," he answered.

"Brother, come to me. I am afraid," said Natalia, and commenced to cry a little.

"Sister," he said, "I try but I cannot. There is something through which I cannot pass. I can see but I cannot press through."

"Can you not climb over, dear Luis?" asked Natalia.

"No, Natalia. I have reached high as I can, but the wall that I cannot see goes up and up."

"Is there no way to get in on the other side of the rock, dear, dear Luis? I am very cold and afraid, being here alone."

"Sister, I have walked around. I have felt high and low. But it is always the same. I cannot get through, I cannot climb over, I cannot crawl under. But I shall stay here with you, so fear not."

At that Natalia put her hands to her face and wept a little, but very quietly, and it pained Luis to see the tears roll down her cheeks and turn to little ice pearls as they fell. After a while Natalia spoke again, but through sobs.

"Brother mine, you heard what the owl said?"

"Yes, sister."

"Does it mean nothing to you?" she asked.

"Nothing," he replied

"But listen," said Natalia. "These were the words: 'Save us from light and the torch's red flame.' "

"I heard that, Natalia. What does it mean?"

"It means, brother, that the things in this horrible valley fear fire. So go, brother. Leave me a while but find fire, coming back with it swiftly. There will be sickening loneliness, so haste, haste."

Hearing that, Luis was sad, for he was in no mood to leave his sister in that plight. Still she urged him, saying: "Speed, brother, speed."

Even then he hesitated, until with a great swoop there passed over the rock a condor wheeling low, and it said as it passed: "Fire will conquer frosted death."

"You hear, brother," said Natalia. "So speed and find fire and return before night."

Then Luis stayed no longer, but waved his sister a farewell and set off down the valley, following the condor that hovered in the air, now darting away and now returning. So Luis knew that the great bird led him, and he ran, presently finding the river and following it until he reached the great vega where the waters met.

At the meeting of the waters he came to a house, a poor thing made of earth and stones snuggled in a warm fold of the hills. No one was about there, but as the condor flew high and, circling in the air, became a small speck, Luis knew that it would be well to stay a while and see what might befall. Pushing open the door he saw by the ashes in the fireplace that someone lived there, for there were red embers well covered to keep the fire alive. So seeing that the owner of the house would return soon, he made himself free of the place, which was the way of that country, and brought fresh water from the spring. Then he gathered wood and piled it neatly by the fireside. Next he blew upon the embers and added twigs and sticks until a bright fire glowed, after which he took the broom of twigs and swept the earth floor clean.

How the man of the house came into the room Luis never knew, but there he was, sitting by the fire on a stool. He looked at things but said nothing to Luis, only nodding his head. Then he brought bread and yerba and offered some to Luis. After they had eaten the old man spoke, and this is what he said:

"Wicked is the white witch, and there is but one way to defeat her. What, lad, is the manner of her defeat? Tell me that."

Then Luis, remembering what the condor had said, repeated the words: " 'Fire will conquer frosted death.' "

"True," said the man slowly, nodding his head. "And your sister is there. Now here comes our friend the condor, who sees far and knows much."

"Now with cold grows faint her breath,
Fire will conquer frosted death."

Having said that the great bird wheeled up sharply.

159

But no sooner was it out of sight than a turkey came running and stood a moment, gobbling. To it the old man gave a lighted brand, repeating the words the condor had spoken.

Off sped the turkey with the blazing stick, running through marsh and swamp in a straight line, and Luis and the old man watched. Soon the bird came to a shallow lagoon, yet made no halt. Straight through the water it sped, and so swiftly that the spray dashed up on either side. High the turkey held the stick, but not high enough, for the splashing water quenched the fire, and seeing that, the bird returned, dropping the blackened stick at the old man's feet.

"Give me another, for the maiden is quivering cold," said the turkey. "This time I will run around the lake."

"No. No," answered the man. "You must know that when the water spirit kisses the fire king, the fire king dies. So, that you may remember, from now and forever you will carry on your feathers the marks of rippling water."

Down again swooped the condor and a little behind him came a goose, flying heavily. As before, the condor cried:

"Now with cold grows faint her breath,
Fire will conquer frosted death,"

then flew away again toward the witch mountain.

To the goose the old man gave a blazing stick and at once the brave bird set off, flying straight in the direction the condor had taken. Over vega and over lagoon she went, pausing only at a snowclad hilltop, because the stick had burned close to her beak. So she dropped it in the snow to get a better hold, and when she picked it up again there was but a charred thing. Sad

160

enough the goose returned to the house, bearing the blackened stick, and begged to be given another chance.

"No. No," said the old man. "The silver snow queen's kiss is death to the fire king. That is something you must remember. From now on and forever you must carry feathers of gray like the ashes. But here comes the condor and we must hear his message."

Sadly then the goose went away, her feathers ash gray, and the condor wheeled low again, calling:

"Fainter grows the maiden's breath,
Night must bring the frosted death,"

and having said, like an arrow he shot off.

No sooner had he gone than the long-legged, long-billed flamingo dropped to the ground.

"Your beak is long," said the old man, "but fly swiftly, for the stick is short."

The flamingo took the burning stick by the end and made straight for the mountain, racing with all possible speed. As for Luis, he made up his mind to tarry no longer and set off, running like a deer. But an ostrich, seeing him, spread her wings like sails and ran by his side. On her back Luis placed his hand, and with that help sped as fast as the flamingo. In the air the flamingo went like an arrow, resting not, although the blazing fire burned her neck and breast until it became pink and red. But that she heeded not. Straight up the valley and to the rock where Natalia was bound went she, and into a heap of dried moss on the south side of the rock she dropped the blazing stick. Up leaped the dancing flames, and with a tremendous noise the rock flew into a thousand pieces and the power of the witch was gone forever. As for Natalia, she was at once freed, and with her gentle, cool hand stroked the breast of the flamingo so that the burns were healed, but as a sign of its bravery the bird has carried a crimson breast from that day to this.

As for Natalia and Luis, they lived for many, many years in the valley, and about them birds of many kinds played and lived and reared their young, and the magic ball of the witch lived only in the memory of men.

❧ Author Biographies ❧

Walter D. Edmonds (1903-1998) claimed that he never really wrote books for children, but rather books for adults and children who like to read. His first novel, *The Matchlock Gun*, a story about frontier survival in America during the eighteenth century, won the Newbery Medal in 1942. He was fond of using the Boonville area of the Mohawk Valley in New York as a setting for his novels, and one of them, *Bert Breen's Barn,* won the National Book Award and the Christopher Award in 1976.

Edmonds wrote about strong characters who are determined to succeed despite the obstacles they must face. He wrote more than twenty-five novels, including the famous *Drums along the Mohawk,* another account of America as it struggled to expand into the frontier.

Born in Boonville, New York, he studied at Harvard University and later returned there to take a position on the Board of Overseers. He lived in Concord, Massachusetts, until his death.

◆ ◆ ◆

Charles J. Finger (1867-1941) was born in Sussex, England. His parents came to the United States in 1887, but he remained in England until 1890, when he joined a ship's crew and sailed for Chile, where he jumped ship. Finger worked herding sheep and guiding tours of the birds of Tierra del Fuego, among other things. By 1896, Finger was a sheep herder in San Angelo, Texas, where he became a U.S. citizen. He married a sheep rancher's daughter, Eleanor Ferguson, with whom he had five children.

Finger founded a music school; wrote newspaper articles; was a railroad general foreman, a railroad company auditor, company director, and general manager; and a magazine editor and publisher. Having lived in Texas, New Mexico, and Ohio, Finger settled in Fayetteville, Arkansas, in 1920 and lived there until his death in 1941.

A frequent traveler, Finger won the Newbery Medal in 1925

for *Tales from Silver Lands,* a collection of South American fantasies, from which our selections are taken. He also won the Longmans Juvenile Fiction Award in 1929 for his book *Courageous Companions.* Finger was the author of more than sixty books of adventure and biography.

◆　◆　◆

Will James (1892-1942) was the cowboy pseudonym for **Joseph Ernest Nepthtali Dufault,** the author of several collections of cowboy stories, which, along with his western adult novels, made up the majority of his fiction output.

A cowboy and rodeo rider himself, James brought the American West alive in his stories, writing in the idiosyncratic dialect of the range cowboy. His depiction of the relationship between the cowboy and his horse, recreated memorably in the Newbery Medal-winning book *Smoky, the Cowhorse,* published in 1926, resurrected an image of the West that was fast dying out. A large part of what made his books so absorbing were his own illustrations, featuring well-muscled horses in powerful, realistic action scenes.

Unfortunately, his past caught up with him. He served a prison sentence for cattle rustling in 1915 before turning to writing, and later, after he wrote his autobiography, it was discovered by outside authenticators that his written life was almost entirely made up, created out of the cowboy illusions that he wrote, ironically, with such realism.

◆　◆　◆

Lois Lenski (1893-1974) is known primarily for her series of middle-school books detailing the lives of everyday American families. Volumes such as **Cotton in My Sack, Shoo-Fly Girl,** and *San Francisco Boy,* respectively, detail the fictional lives of a Southern sharecropper girl, a Pennsylvania Amish girl, and a Chinese-American boy living in San Francisco. In 1946, the

Newbery Medal was awarded to Lenski's book, *Strawberry Girl,* which tells about a girl named Birdie and her family as they start a strawberry farm in Florida. These books are made all the more real by the author's exhaustive research into the lives of these various regional groups of people, often including visits to see their day-to-day activities in person.

Born in Springfield, Ohio, Lenski earned a B.S. in education from Ohio State University, then went on to study at the Art Students' League in New York and the prestigious Westminster School of Art in London. Right after school, she married the artist Arthur Covey and raised their son and two stepchildren with him until his death in 1960. Her artwork garnered her several single artist shows, notably a display of oil paintings in the Weyhe Gallery and a watercolors show in the Ferargils Gallery, both in New York. She also was included in group art shows at the Pennsylvania Water Color Show and the New York Water Color Show.

During her lifetime, she wrote more than one hundred books of stories, poetry, and plays, the majority of them illustrated by her as well. Her autobiography, *Journey into Childhood,* was finished two years before her death.

◆ ◆ ◆

Robin McKinley (1952-) is known for her imaginative retellings of classic fairy tales, rich and diverse original fantasy novels, adaptations of works such as *Black Beauty* and *The Jungle Book Stories,* and well-crafted, award-winning anthologies. Her novels are marked by strong female characters whose growth and maturity are focal points of her work. McKinley's rich writing style also captivates readers.

McKinley was born in Warren, Ohio, in 1952. Her father was in the navy, so the family traveled and lived all over the world. In 1975, she graduated summa cum laude from Maine's Bowdoin College. Three years later, the first publisher to which McKinley sent her first novel, *Beauty,* accepted it.

Her fantasy novel *The Hero and the Crown* won the Newbery

Medal in 1985. Her work has also won several other awards, including the World Fantasy Award for Best Anthology for *Imaginary Lands,* and Horn Book Honor List and American Library Association Notable Book recognition for *Beauty: A Retelling of the Story of Beauty and the Beast.*

Before turning to freelance writing, McKinley worked in a variety of careers, including being an editorial assistant at Little, Brown, and Company; clerking in a bookstore; and managing a Massachusetts horse farm. Currently she lives with her writer husband, Peter Dickinson, in Hampshire, England.

❦ Newbery Award-Winning Books ❦

2001
WINNER:
A Year Down Yonder by Richard Peck

HONOR BOOKS:
Hope Was Here by Joan Bauer
The Wanderer by Sharon Creech
Because of Winn-Dixie
by Kate DiCamillo
Joey Pigza Loses Control
by Jack Gantos

2000
WINNER:
Bud, Not Buddy
by Christopher Paul Curtis

HONOR BOOKS:
Getting Near to Baby
by Audrey Couloumbis
Our Only May Amelia
by Jennifer L. Holm
26 Fairmount Avenue
by Tomie dePaola

1999
WINNER:
Holes by Louis Sachar

HONOR BOOK:
A Long Way from Chicago
by Richard Peck

1998
WINNER:
Out of the Dust by Karen Hesse

HONOR BOOKS:
Ella Enchanted by Gail Carson Levine
Lily's Crossing by Patricia Reilly Giff
Wringer by Jerry Spinelli

1997
WINNER:
The View from Saturday
by E.L. Konigsburg

HONOR BOOKS:
Belle Prater's Boy by Ruth White
A Girl Named Disaster
by Nancy Farmer
Moorchild by Eloise McGraw
The Thief by Megan Whalen Turner

1996
WINNER:
The Midwife's Apprentice
by Karen Cushman

HONOR BOOKS:
The Great Fire by Jim Murphy
*The Watsons Go to
Birmingham — 1963*
by Christopher Paul Curtis
What Jamie Saw by Carolyn Coman
Yolanda's Genius by Carol Fenner

1995
WINNER:
Walk Two Moons
by Sharon Creech

HONOR BOOKS:
Catherine, Called Birdy
by Karen Cushman
The Ear, the Eye, and the Arm
by Nancy Farmer

1994
WINNER:
The Giver by Lois Lowry

HONOR BOOKS:
Crazy Lady by Jane Leslie Conly
Dragon's Gate by Laurence Yep
*Eleanor Roosevelt:
A Life of Discovery*
by Russell Freedman

1993
WINNER:
Missing May by Cynthia Rylant

HONOR BOOKS:
The Dark-thirty: Southern
Tales of the Supernatural
by Patricia McKissack
Somewhere in the Darkness
by Walter Dean Myers
What Hearts by Bruce Brooks

1992

WINNER:
Shiloh by Phyllis Reynolds Naylor

HONOR BOOKS:
Nothing But the Truth:
A Documentary Novel
by Avi
The Wright Brothers: How They
Invented the Airplane
by Russell Freedman

1991

WINNER:
Maniac Magee by Jerry Spinelli

HONOR BOOK:
The True Confessions of
Charlotte Doyle
by Avi

1990

WINNER:
Number the Stars by Lois Lowry

HONOR BOOKS:
Afternoon of the Elves
by Janet Taylor Lisle
Shabanu, Daughter of the Wind
by Suzanne Fisher Staples
The Winter Room by Gary Paulsen

1989

WINNER:
Joyful Noise: Poems for Two Voices
by Paul Fleischman

HONOR BOOKS:
In the Beginning: Creation Stories
from around the World
by Virginia Hamilton
Scorpions by Walter Dean Myers

1988

WINNER:
Lincoln: A Photobiography
by Russell Freedman

HONOR BOOKS:
After the Rain
by Norma Fox Mazer
Hatchet by Gary Paulsen

1987

WINNER:
The Whipping Boy by Sid Fleischman

HONOR BOOKS:
A Fine White Dust by Cynthia Rylant
On My Honor by Marion Dane Bauer
Volcano: The Eruption and
Healing of Mount St. Helens
by Patricia Lauber

1986

WINNER:
Sarah, Plain and Tall
by Patricia MacLachlan

HONOR BOOKS:
Commodore Perry in the
Land of the Shogun
by Rhonda Blumberg
Dogsong by Gary Paulsen

1985

WINNER:
The Hero and the Crown
by Robin McKinley

HONOR BOOKS:
Like Jake and Me by Mavis Jukes
The Moves Make the Man
by Bruce Brooks
One-Eyed Cat by Paula Fox

1984

WINNER:
Dear Mr. Henshaw by Beverly Cleary

HONOR BOOKS:
The Sign of the Beaver
by Elizabeth George Speare

A Solitary Blue by Cynthia Voigt

Sugaring Time by Kathryn Lasky

The Wish Giver: Three Tales of Coven Tree by Bill Brittain

1983

WINNER:
Dicey's Song by Cynthia Voigt

HONOR BOOKS:
The Blue Sword by Robin McKinley

Doctor DeSoto by William Steig

Graven Images by Paul Fleischman

Homesick: My Own Story by Jean Fritz

Sweet Whispers, Brother Rush by Virginia Hamilton

1982

WINNER:
A Visit to William Blake's Inn: Poems for Innocent and Experienced Travelers by Nancy Willard

HONOR BOOKS:
Ramona Quimby, Age 8 by Beverly Cleary

Upon the Head of the Goat: A Childhood in Hungary 1939-1944 by Aranka Siegal

1981

WINNER:
Jacob Have I Loved by Katherine Paterson

HONOR BOOKS:
The Fledgling by Jane Langton

A Ring of Endless Light by Madeleine L'Engle

1980

WINNER:
A Gathering of Days: A New England Girl's Journal, 1830-1832 by Joan W. Blos

HONOR BOOK:
The Road from Home: The Story of an Armenian Girl by David Kherdian

1979

WINNER:
The Westing Game by Ellen Raskin

HONOR BOOK:
The Great Gilly Hopkins by Katherine Paterson

1978

WINNER:
Bridge to Terabithia by Katherine Paterson

HONOR BOOKS:
Anpao: An American Indian Odyssey by Jamake Highwater

Ramona and Her Father by Beverly Cleary

1977

WINNER:
Roll of Thunder, Hear My Cry by Mildred D. Taylor

HONOR BOOKS:
Abel's Island by William Steig

A String in the Harp by Nancy Bond

1976

WINNER:
The Grey King by Susan Cooper

HONOR BOOKS:
Dragonwings by Laurence Yep

The Hundred Penny Box by Sharon Bell Mathis

1975

WINNER:
M.C. Higgins, the Great by Virginia Hamilton

HONOR BOOKS:
Figgs & Phantoms by Ellen Raskin

My Brother Sam Is Dead
by James Lincoln Collier
and Christopher Collier

The Perilous Gard
by Elizabeth Marie Pope

*Philip Hall Likes Me, I
Reckon Maybe*
by Bette Greene

1974

WINNER:
The Slave Dancer by Paula Fox

HONOR BOOK:
The Dark Is Rising by Susan Cooper

1973

WINNER:
Julie of the Wolves
by Jean Craighead George

HONOR BOOKS:
Frog and Toad Together
by Arnold Lobel

The Upstairs Room by Johanna Reiss

The Witches of Worm
by Zilpha Keatley Snyder

1972

WINNER:
Mrs. Frisby and the Rats of NIMH
by Robert C. O'Brien

HONOR BOOKS:
Annie and the Old One
by Miska Miles

The Headless Cupid
by Zilpha Keatley Snyder

Incident at Hawk's Hill
by Allan W. Eckert

The Planet of Junior Brown
by Virginia Hamilton

The Tombs of Atuan
by Ursula K. Le Guin

1971

WINNER:
Summer of the Swans by Betsy Byars

HONOR BOOKS:
Enchantress from the Stars
by Sylvia Louise Engdahl

Knee Knock Rise by Natalie Babbitt

Sing Down the Moon by Scott O'Dell

1970

WINNER:
Sounder by William H. Armstrong

HONOR BOOKS:
Journey Outside by Mary Q. Steele

*The Many Ways of Seeing:
An Introduction to the
Pleasures of Art*
by Janet Gaylord Moore

Our Eddie by Sulamith Ish-Kishor

1969

WINNER:
The High King by Lloyd Alexander

HONOR BOOKS:
To Be a Slave by Julius Lester

*When Shlemiel Went to Warsaw
and Other Stories*
by Isaac Bashevis Singer

1968

WINNER:
*From the Mixed-Up Files of
Mrs. Basil E. Frankweiler*
by E.L. Konigsburg

HONOR BOOKS:
The Black Pearl
by Scott O'Dell

The Egypt Game
by Zilpha Keatley Snyder

The Fearsome Inn
by Isaac Bashevis Singer

*Jennifer, Hecate, Macbeth, William
McKinley, and Me, Elizabeth*
by E.L. Konigsburg

1967

WINNER:
Up a Road Slowly by Irene Hunt

The Jazz Man by Mary Hays Weik

The King's Fifth by Scott O'Dell

Zlateh the Goat and Other Stories
by Isaac Bashevis Singer

1966

WINNER:

I, Juan de Pareja
by Elizabeth Borton de Trevino

HONOR BOOKS:

The Animal Family by Randall Jarrell

The Black Cauldron
by Lloyd Alexander

The Noonday Friends by Mary Stolz

1965

WINNER:

Shadow of a Bull
by Maia Wojciechowska

HONOR BOOK:

Across Five Aprils by Irene Hunt

1964

WINNER:

It's Like This, Cat by Emily Neville

HONOR BOOKS:

The Loner by Ester Wier

Rascal: A Memoir of a Better Era
by Sterling North

1963

WINNER:

A Wrinkle in Time
by Madeleine L'Engle

HONOR BOOKS:

Men of Athens by Olivia Coolidge

*Thistle and Thyme: Tales and
Legends from Scotland*
by Sorche Nic Leodhas

1962

WINNER:

The Bronze Bow
by Elizabeth George Speare

HONOR BOOKS:

Belling the Tiger by Mary Stolz

Frontier Living by Edwin Tunis

The Golden Goblet
by Eloise Jarvis McGraw

1961

WINNER:

Island of the Blue Dolphins
by Scott O'Dell

HONOR BOOKS:

*America Moves Forward:
A History for Peter*
by Gerald W. Johnson

The Cricket in Times Square
by George Selden

Old Ramon by Jack Schaefer

1960

WINNER:

Onion John by Joseph Krumgold

HONOR BOOKS:

*America Is Born:
A History for Peter*
by Gerald W. Johnson

The Gammage Cup by Carol Kendall

My Side of the Mountain
by Jean Craighead George

1959

WINNER:

The Witch of Blackbird Pond
by Elizabeth George Speare

HONOR BOOKS:

Along Came a Dog
by Meindert DeJong

Chucaro: Wild Pony of the Pampa
by Francis Kalnay

The Family Under the Bridge
by Natalie Savage Carlson

The Perilous Road by William O. Steele

1958

WINNER:

Rifles for Watie by Harold Keith

HONOR BOOKS:

Gone-Away Lake
by Elizabeth Enright

The Great Wheel
by Robert Lawson

The Horsecatcher by Mari Sandoz

Tom Paine, Freedom's Apostle
by Leo Gurko

1957

WINNER:

Miracles on Maple Hill
by Virginia Sorenson

HONOR BOOKS:

Black Fox of Lorne
by Marguerite de Angeli

The Corn Grows Ripe
by Dorothy Rhoads

The House of Sixty Fathers
by Meindert DeJong

Mr. Justice Holmes
by Clara Ingram Judson

Old Yeller by Fred Gipson

1956

WINNER:

Carry On, Mr. Bowditch
by Jean Lee Latham

HONOR BOOKS:

The Golden Name Day
by Jennie Lindquist

*Men, Microscopes, and
Living Things*
by Katherine Shippen

The Secret River
by Marjorie Kinnan Rawlings

1955

WINNER:

The Wheel on the School
by Meindert DeJong

HONOR BOOKS:

Banner in the Sky
by James Ullman

Courage of Sarah Noble
by Alice Dalgliesh

1954

WINNER:

. . . And Now Miguel
by Joseph Krumgold

HONOR BOOKS:

All Alone by Claire Huchet Bishop

Hurry Home, Candy
by Meindert DeJong

Magic Maize by Mary and Conrad Buff

Shadrach by Meindert DeJong

Theodore Roosevelt, Fighting Patriot
by Clara Ingram Judson

1953

WINNER:

Secret of the Andes by Ann Nolan Clark

HONOR BOOKS:

The Bears on Hemlock Mountain
by Alice Dalgliesh

Birthdays of Freedom, Vol. 1
by Genevieve Foster

Charlotte's Web by E.B. White

Moccasin Trail by Eloise McGraw

Red Sails to Capri by Ann Weil

1952

WINNER:

Ginger Pye by Eleanor Estes

HONOR BOOKS:

Americans Before Columbus
by Elizabeth Baity

The Apple and the Arrow
by Mary and Conrad Buff

The Defender by Nicholas Kalashnikoff

The Light at Tern Rock by Julia Sauer

Minn of the Mississippi
by Holling C. Holling

1951

WINNER:

Amos Fortune, Free Man
by Elizabeth Yates

HONOR BOOKS:

Abraham Lincoln, Friend of the People
by Clara Ingram Judson

Better Known as Johnny Appleseed
by Mabel Leigh Hunt

Gandhi, Fighter without a Sword
by Jeanette Eaton

The Story of Appleby Capple
by Anne Parrish

1950

WINNER:
The Door in the Wall
by Marguerite de Angeli

HONOR BOOKS:
The Blue Cat of Castle Town
by Catherine Coblentz

George Washington
by Genevieve Foster

Kildee House
by Rutherford Montgomery

*Song of the Pines: A Story of
Norwegian Lumbering in Wisconsin*
by Walter and Marion Havighurst

Tree of Freedom by Rebecca Caudill

1949

WINNER:
King of the Wind by Marguerite Henry

HONOR BOOKS:
Daughter of the Mountain
by Louise Rankin

My Father's Dragon
by Ruth S. Gannett

Seabird by Holling C. Holling

Story of the Negro by Arna Bontemps

1948

WINNER:
The Twenty-One Balloons
by William Pène du Bois

HONOR BOOKS:
*The Cow-Tail Switch, and
Other West African Stories*
by Harold Courlander

Li Lun, Lad of Courage
by Carolyn Treffinger

Misty of Chincoteague
by Marguerite Henry

Pancakes-Paris by Claire Huchet Bishop

*The Quaint and Curious Quest
of Johnny Longfoot*
by Catherine Besterman

1947

WINNER:
Miss Hickory by Carolyn Sherwin Bailey

HONOR BOOKS:
The Avion My Uncle Flew
by Cyrus Fisher

Big Tree by Mary and Conrad Buff

The Heavenly Tenants
by William Maxwell

The Hidden Treasure of Glaston
by Eleanor Jewett

Wonderful Year by Nancy Barnes

1946

WINNER:
Strawberry Girl by Lois Lenski

HONOR BOOKS:
Bhimsa, the Dancing Bear
by Christine Weston

Justin Morgan Had a Horse
by Marguerite Henry

The Moved-Outers
by Florence Crannell Means

New Found World by Katherine Shippen

1945

WINNER:
Rabbit Hill by Robert Lawson

HONOR BOOKS:
Abraham Lincoln's World
by Genevieve Foster

The Hundred Dresses by Eleanor Estes

*Lone Journey: The Life of
Roger Williams*
by Jeanette Eaton

The Silver Pencil by Alice Dalgliesh

1944

WINNER:
Johnny Tremain by Esther Forbes

Fog Magic by Julia Sauer

Mountain Born by Elizabeth Yates

Rufus M. by Eleanor Estes

These Happy Golden Years
by Laura Ingalls Wilder

1943

WINNER:
Adam of the Road
by Elizabeth Janet Gray

HONOR BOOKS:
Have You Seen Tom Thumb?
by Mabel Leigh Hunt

The Middle Moffat by Eleanor Estes

1942

WINNER:
The Matchlock Gun
by Walter D. Edmonds

HONOR BOOKS:
Down Ryton Water
by Eva Roe Gaggin

George Washington's World
by Genevieve Foster

*Indian Captive: The Story
of Mary Jemison*
by Lois Lenski

Little Town on the Prairie
by Laura Ingalls Wilder

1941

WINNER:
Call It Courage by Armstrong Sperry

HONOR BOOKS:
Blue Willow by Doris Gates

The Long Winter
by Laura Ingalls Wilder

Nansen by Anna Gertrude Hall

Young Mac of Fort Vancouver
by Mary Jane Carr

1940

WINNER:
Daniel Boone by James Daugherty

HONOR BOOKS:
Boy with a Pack
by Stephen W. Meader

By the Shores of Silver Lake
by Laura Ingalls Wilder

*Runner of the Mountain Tops:
The Life of Louis Agassiz*
by Mabel Robinson

The Singing Tree by Kate Seredy

1939

WINNER:
Thimble Summer by Elizabeth Enright

HONOR BOOKS:
Hello the Boat! by Phyllis Crawford

*Leader by Destiny: George
Washington, Man and Patriot*
by Jeanette Eaton

Mr. Popper's Penguins
by Richard and Florence Atwater

Nino by Valenti Angelo

Penn by Elizabeth Janet Gray

1938

WINNER:
The White Stag by Kate Seredy

HONOR BOOKS:
Bright Island by Mabel Robinson

On the Banks of Plum Creek
by Laura Ingalls Wilder

Pecos Bill by James Cloyd Bowman

1937

WINNER:
Roller Skates by Ruth Sawyer

HONOR BOOKS:
Audubon by Constance Rourke

The Codfish Musket by Agnes Hewes

The Golden Basket
by Ludwig Bemelmans

Phoebe Fairchild: Her Book
by Lois Lenski

Whistler's Van by Idwal Jones

Winterbound by Margery Bianco

1936

WINNER:
Caddie Woodlawn by Carol Ryrie Brink

HONOR BOOKS:
All Sail Set: A Romance of the Flying Cloud
by Armstrong Sperry

The Good Master by Kate Seredy

Honk, the Moose by Phil Stong

Young Walter Scott
by Elizabeth Janet Gray

1935

WINNER:
Dobry by Monica Shannon

HONOR BOOKS:
Davy Crockett by Constance Rourke

Days on Skates: The Story of a Dutch Picnic
by Hilda Von Stockum

Pageant of Chinese History
by Elizabeth Seeger

1934

WINNER:
Invincible Louisa: The Story of the Author of Little Women
by Cornelia Meigs

HONOR BOOKS:
ABC Bunny by Wanda Gág

Apprentice of Florence by Ann Kyle

Big Tree of Bunlahy: Stories of My Own Countryside
by Padraic Colum

The Forgotten Daughter
by Caroline Snedeker

Glory of the Seas by Agnes Hewes

New Land by Sarah Schmidt

Swords of Steel by Elsie Singmaster

Winged Girl of Knossos by Erik Berry

1933

WINNER:
Young Fu of the Upper Yangtze
by Elizabeth Lewis

HONOR BOOKS:
Children of the Soil: A Story of Scandinavia
by Nora Burglon

The Railroad to Freedom: A Story of the Civil War
by Hildegarde Swift

Swift Rivers by Cornelia Meigs

1932

WINNER:
Waterless Mountain
by Laura Adams Armer

HONOR BOOKS:
Boy of the South Seas
by Eunice Tietjens

Calico Bush by Rachel Field

The Fairy Circus
by Dorothy P. Lathrop

Jane's Island by Marjorie Allee

Out of the Flame by Eloise Lownsbery

Truce of the Wolf and Other Tales of Old Italy
by Mary Gould Davis

1931

WINNER:
The Cat Who Went to Heaven
by Elizabeth Coatsworth

HONOR BOOKS:
The Dark Star of Itza: The Story of a Pagan Princess
by Alida Malkus

Floating Island by Anne Parrish

Garram the Hunter: A Boy of the Hill Tribes
by Herbert Best

Meggy Macintosh
by Elizabeth Janet Gray

Mountains Are Free
by Julia Davis Adams

Ood-Le-Uk the Wanderer
by Alice Lide and Margaret Johansen

Queer Person by Ralph Hubbard

Spice and the Devil's Cake
by Agnes Hewes

1930

WINNER:
Hitty, Her First Hundred Years
by Rachel Field

HONOR BOOKS:
A Daughter of the Seine: The Life of Madam Roland
by Jeanette Eaton

Jumping-Off Place
by Marian Hurd McNeely

Little Blacknose by Hildegarde Swift

Pran of Albania by Elizabeth Miller

The Tangle-Coated Horse and Other Tales
by Ella Young

Vaino by Julia Davis Adams

1929

WINNER:
The Trumpeter of Krakow
by Eric P. Kelly

HONOR BOOKS:
The Boy Who Was by Grace Hallock

Clearing Weather
by Cornelia Meigs

Millions of Cats by Wanda Gág

Pigtail of Ah Lee Ben Loo
by John Bennett

Runaway Papoose
by Grace Moon

Tod of the Fens by Elinor Whitney

1928

WINNER:
Gay Neck, the Story of a Pigeon
by Dhan Gopal Mukerji

HONOR BOOKS:
Downright Dencey
by Caroline Snedeker

The Wonder Smith and His Son
by Ella Young

1927

WINNER:
Smoky, the Cowhorse by Will James

1926

WINNER:
Shen of the Sea
by Arthur Bowie Chrisman

HONOR BOOK:
The Voyagers: Being Legends and Romances of Atlantic Discovery
by Padraic Colum

1925

WINNER:
Tales from Silver Lands
by Charles Finger

HONOR BOOKS:
The Dream Coach by Anne Parrish

Nicholas: A Manhattan Christmas Story
by Annie Carroll Moore

1924

WINNER:
The Dark Frigate
by Charles Boardman Hawes

1923

WINNER:
The Voyages of Doctor Doolittle
by Hugh Lofting

1922

WINNER:
The Story of Mankind
by Hendrik Willem van Loon

HONOR BOOKS:
Cedric the Forester
by Bernard Marshall

The Golden Fleece and the Heroes Who Lived Before Achilles
by Padraic Colum

The Great Quest
by Charles Boardman Hawes

The Old Tobacco Shop: A True Account of What Befell a Little Boy in Search of Adventure
by William Bowen

The Windy Hill by Cornelia Meigs